Letters of an Irish Parish Priest

JOHN B. KEANE

THE MERCIER PRESS
4 BRIDGE STREET, CORK

© John B. Keane
First published 1972
Reprinted 1973
Reprinted 1974
Reprinted 1975
Reprinted 1976
Reprinted 1978
Reprinted 1980

ISBN 0 85342 294 X

LETTERS OF AN IRISH PARISH PRIEST

The Presbytery,
Lochnanane.

Dear Joe,

I've just come in from the garden where I spent the
morning planting daffodil bulbs. The man before me, the
late Father John Clement Fitzraymond used to claim
relationship with Strongbow. He had a book of sermons
published by Shule and Rune, the London firm and he
had his suits made in Saville Row. There is a garden
in front of the presbytery consisting of one acre and
thirteen roods, yet in all his fourteen years as parish
priest of Lochnanane he failed to plant one daffodil.
Have no fear but he planted the bulbs of doubt in the
collective crania of The Lochnanaanites. After nearly a
year I am still trying to re-establish contact with the
ordinary people.

God in his wisdom has whistled many a strange
warbler into the church but did you ever hear of a
priest who charged a guinea for saying Mass, who, the
year before he died addressed the final year students
in Saint Olack's with the opening question 'Stand up all
here who masturbate.' Needless to mention no-one
stood up. This then is the man in whose wake I must
navigate, whose potholes I must fill in, whose hedges
trim as it were. This is the man who introduced grapefruit to the parish of Lochnanane. By this he is
remembered and by nothing else.

He brought the grapefruit in a brown paper bag from
the city of Cork when he was a curate at this place
in 1937. He bamboozled poor Norrie Crean who was
housekeeper at the time.

'Oh Lord Jaysus,' said she. 'That's the size of an
orange. 'Tis as big as an elephant's conundrum.' The
same Lord have mercy on Norrie and all the poor

innocent souls this hallowed month of November. I offered Mass for your mother this morning. I know you miss her more than I although she was my only sister. She is surely in heaven. Yes, indeed. She is in heaven or there is nobody there.

The new curate arrived this morning. He seems a likeable sort, nicely disposed and well-mannered. I suppose you could call him self-effacing. Time will tell. His senior, Father Romane is still the same. He has as much integrity as a certain English Sunday newspaper. The last thing I want to be is harsh and on that account I'll say no more. He is due to depart in a few days and please God the memory of him will be shortlived. I don't envy his new parish priest. Mary Teresa was never better. She sends her regards.

Do you want for anything? Let me know your needs when next you write and don't spare me. This is a good parish in that respect.

Affectionately,
Your uncle,
Martin O'Mora, P.P.

•   g   a   ‹   g   •   •   •   •   •   •

The Willows,
Gurtacreen,
Lochnanane.

Dear Father O'Mora,

I called twice but you were out on each occasion. Let me introduce myself. I am Henry Dring, a native of this place, who is now home to stay after forty years in exile. I bought this fine house some months ago but only took up residence a fortnight back. I am a retired headmaster, widowed and without family. I had better come to the point and in so doing would have you remember that it is from a sense of duty and nothing else that I am compelled to unfold the following harrowing tale; as you will recall, the second fortnight of

October was exceptionally fine. The last Monday of the month, in particular, was more like a June day than an October one. I motored in the afternoon to the beach known as Trawbofin four miles from here and set out for a walk across the dunes. There were few about; an elderly couple as I recall and a mother or governess with some children far up the beach. Suddenly a young couple dashed from behind a sandhill and ran towards the sea. You will say to yourself that they were perfectly entitled to do so. I concur and I would fight to the death for their right to dash into the sea provided they were wearing bathing attire, however immodest that attire might be.

I regret to inform you that they wore nothing whatso-ever. They ran past me shamelessly, ignoring me even when I called after them in protest. The only words that escaped the young man's lips were when he admini-stered a half-hearted slap to the girl's bare buttocks – I recall what he said: 'Get moving or get mounted, your posterior has me intoxicated.'

I left the dunes in disgust vowing never to return until they were made safe for God-fearing people.

I naturally assumed that this immoral couple were from some distant city or foreign land forsaken by God, such as England or Wales. Some weeks later I was shocked to discover that the young man is a teacher in Lochnanane. Worse still the girl works in a chemist's shop here. You can imagine my feeling of outrage at this gruesome discovery. My first thought was to report the matter to the Civic Guards but I decided, before doing so, that you should know first. The young man's name is Thomas Cooley. Being a gentleman I will not mention the girl's. I hope to hear from you soon regard-ing this most serious matter.

Sincerely,
Henry Dring, M.A.

•   •   •   ᵹ   ᵹ   ᵹ   ˉ   ᵹ   •   •   •

St. Unshin's College,
Ballyrango.

Dear Uncle Martin,

Many thanks for your letter. Funny you should mention daffodils. The three new girl students here spent all yesterday afternoon planting daffodils and irises with the junior dean, Father Mockessy. The new girls are the talk of the place. By and large the students are in favour of having them but the entire teaching staff, Mockessy excepted, are in a dither and don't even know how to behave towards them. You could call it 'conservatism at the crossroads.' The president, Monsignor Dang, pretends they aren't there at all and I'm sure he's secretly hoping they'll just go away. It wouldn't be so bad if they were nuns but three attractive laywomen out of the blue is a bit much for the college elders.

I had a short note from my father to say that he would be in Ireland for a spell before Christmas with his friend Mrs. Garrett. He said he would like to see me so I told him it would be alright if they wanted to stay overnight in one of the guesthouses here in Ballyrango. I hope you don't mind. Whatever else he is my father. I know you can't stand him and I know you have good reason or you wouldn't treat him the way you do. Don't you think it's time you told me. You are the nearest person I have in this world. There is no-one else really. I have my own reasons for not caring one way or the other about my father. I am more interested in yours as they would weigh more heavily with me. I will be twenty-one in less than a week and I am a bachelor of arts. What I am trying to say is that I feel I can be trusted with any confidence, that I am mature enough and resilient enough to be able to absorb any heavy data which I might hitherto have been incapable of doing.

I got a tip for a horse called Finicky Fencer from a pal of mine here. His father is a trainer and thinks this horse will win in a two mile maiden chase at Limerick Junction next Thursday. Have two pounds each way

8

for me and I'll settle up with you in due course. Have a flutter yourself and tell Mary Teresa.

I'll close now. We are rehearsing a show for after Christmas and I have a small part.

> Your affectionate nephew,
> Joseph.

◼   ◼   ◼   ◾   ◾   ◦   ◦   ◦   •   •   •

> The Presbytery,
> Lochnanane.

Dear Joe,

That was solid information about Finicky Fencer. I hold your winnings. Mary Teresa and I had a bet and collected. It's you that's in for the good feeding at Christmas. I have been confronted with a thorny problem since I wrote to you last.

A Henry Dring wrote first and then called to complain about young Tom Cooley, one of my teachers, and a certain young lady. Dring asserts that he saw Tom and the girl in the nude at the strand of Trawbofin in the middle of your noon day. I don't doubt it but so long as no one was scandalised I do not see how it could be the concern of anybody. Dring, who is a retired headmaster and whose mother came from these parts, has threatened to go to the Civic Guards and I may tell you that this would not do at all.

I am very fond of young Tom Cooley and he is also an excellent teacher. This fellow Dring must be made to retract. He had an uncle, his mother's brother, Canon Dring of Killaveg, who had the reputation of being the second meanest parish priest ever to hold office in the diocese. Old Canon Dring died from malnutrition but not before he salted five thousand quid over on the sister. This is how our present Mr. Dring got his M.A.

While oul' Dring was P.P. of Killaveg there was a Tom Kilmartin, a pal of mine, a curate there. Tom told me that there was only one W.C. in the presbytery,

9

It consisted of a cracked toilet bowl and a flush tank that never worked. Tom was never permitted to use the toilet. This was reserved for oul' Dring. Whenever Tom had a call of nature he had to go behind the house. He was lucky in this regard because behind was a large uneven bog which afforded him a change of scenery every time he wanted to release a button. He was often caught in the act by a turfcutter or a stray tourist. To this day when he enters a bathroom or W.C. he looks behind him regularly expecting to be surprised.

Nellie Dwan, the housekeeper, was not allowed to use the W.C. either but she had an outsize enamel chamber pot which she bought at an auction. This she faithfully emptied every morning in a stream about two hundred yards from the presbytery. She was frequently followed by schoolboys who would ask her if the pot was full or if it was to the creamery she was going and so forth and so on. She was often mortified. The people of the parish could always tell by her gait if the pot was full or half full or near empty. If she walked slow, one neighbour might remark to another 'By the Lord but poor Nellie Dwan had a lively night last night,' or if the pot was near empty 'By the Lord but Nellie Dwan must have wet the tick last night.'

Anyhow I have summoned Tom Cooley to render an account of himself. It should be an interesting interview.

So your father is coming before Christmas with Mrs. Garrett his so-called wife. How in the name of God can she be called a wife whose husband and children are still to the good. I'll grant you she is divorced and that her children are grown up and that her ass of a husband married again but she has no religion of any kind. She isn't even a Protestant. Your father is a Catholic and yet he married in a registry office in London. He can say what he likes and she can say what she likes but in the sight of God they are not married. They are adulterers. I'll say no more about them.

I hope all is well with you. Being a Third Divine is a happy time. Soon you will be a Subdeacon D.V. It was my favourite year at Saint Unshin's. Those few girls around the place will do no harm – they'll liven things up – it would have been considered a sacrilege in my day.

Joe, there were many wrongs in my time but the passage of the years, thank God, has set most of them to rights. There is one thing I find it hard to forgive myself for.

When I was a young priest it was fashionable to waylay young courting couples and pairs of lovers in the laneways and out-of-the-way places at night. We often surprised and chastised older lovers in great need of each other. As God is my judge Joe I don't know why I did it? It was the fashion. That's all I can say in defence of myself.

I know why some did it. It was because they were lonely themselves and had natural longings and many found release in this sort of persecution. It still goes on sporadically and it will always go on I suppose but Joe, believe me when I say, it is one of the very few things that I have ever been ashamed of.

You ask me to explain my dislike of your father. You are now old enough to know. It has little to do with his obsession with that grey-haired trollop Mrs. Garrett.

After you were born Joe the doctor told your mother that she was to have no more children. He was most emphatic about it and he pointed out that should she conceive again she would be placing her life in grave danger. Your mother was one of the most perfect Catholics I have ever known. Only God knows how good that woman really was.

It was put to your father that he should sleep with your mother no longer. She was unpredictable in her menstruals which made the risk even greater. He agreed but he broke his word and in a matter of months your poor mother was expecting another child. The doctor was pessimistic but I saw to it that the best specialists in the field were available.

Your father suggested an abortion. I could have struck him. Your mother was appalled. To her and to me such a course was unthinkable. As the days passed and the time of her confinement drew near your father

11

began to insist that there be an abortion. He even went to a solicitor. What's the point in labouring the issue. My heart aches even now when I remember.

She died in childbirth. Everything possible was done to save her. It was all to no avail. I closed her eyes on the bitterest morning of my life. The child died a few days later. Your father threatened to kill me. After a few weeks he left and it was five years before I heard from him. That was when he tried to claim you. He hadn't a leg to stand on.

He is your father. You must never forget that. You must never forget your mother either. Time has dimmed a lot of things for me but the ache in my heart which came after your mother died has never left. It never will. Let us have no more of this particular subject but let us look to the brighter days ahead. Write soon.

Affectionately,
Your Uncle,
Martin O'Mora, P.P.

P.S. (The new curate is a grand lad – more of him anon.)

. . . .

The Presbytery,
Lochnanane.

Dear Dring,

Sorry to have been out when you called. I was on a sick call and while I am parish priest of Lochnanane sick calls will always have priority no matter who may ordain otherwise.

Should you ever feel like calling again it might be a good idea to drop me a note. I cannot be expected to sit inside all day awaiting casual callers. We also have a phone in the house, Lochnanane 2. Why not ring and advise me as to the approximate time of your next arrival. This would greatly facilitate me and any-

12

way I am most anxious to meet the man who makes the most monstrous accusations ever to assail my ears.

I am also anxious to meet the nephew of the late Canon Henry Dring of whom I have heard so much over the years.

Like I say, sir, a note or a ring on the phone would be the intelligent thing to do.

Now let us come to your letter and the apparition you claim you saw on the strand of Trawbofin. Let me tell you that I have not yet acquainted Mr. Thomas Cooley of your accusation. I am not such a fool. I have known Mr. Cooley for three years as a teacher and for twenty-one as a person. Be assured sir that he is a devout Catholic, an excellent teacher and the youngest son of a family of seven distinguished males and four equally distinguished females.

What the hell were you on the look-out for anyway? Are there no birds on the great strand of Trawbofin, no cadaverous cormorants clutching the glinting rocks, no oyster catchers conning the clear shallows, no air-loving plovers ploughing the unimpeachable elements?

What does one look for on an October seashore? I would ask you to think before you answer. It is possible you saw a young couple without clothes. What if you did. By your own admission it was a broiling day and by your own admission the couple you saw were young. You were a mere witness to a classical natural reaction. It is your mind sir that needs to be clothed, not the innocent bodies of God's children.

You say that a man you believe to be Thomas Cooley threatened to mount the girl if she did not get a move on. I am at a loss for words in the face of the other expression you used. I am seeing Mr. Thomas Cooley tomorrow and if you wish you may make the accusation to his face.

Yours in J C.
Martin O'Mora, P.P.

.   .   .   .

The Willows,
Gurtacreen,
Lochnanane.

Dear Father O'Mora,

I have no wish to be present when you interrogate Mr.
Thomas Cooley. When I call to the Guards' Barracks
I will, if he is present, make such an accusation to his
face and to the face of the girl.

Before I go to the Guards I want to assure you that
I am merely doing my Christian duty and that I am not
the dirty-minded person you try to make me out to be.
I am a reasonable man, travelled and broadminded. I
will postpone my visit to the Guards until I hear from
you again. Then I must go and no power on earth will
stop me.

Yours faithfully,
Henry Dring, M.A.

•   •   •   •   •   •   •   •   •   •   •

St. Unshin's College,
Ballyrango.

Dear Uncle Martin,

I read your letter with great interest and I am grateful
that you explained your position with regard to my
father. How could he have been so monstrous. How
in the name of all that is just and holy could he con-
template such a thing. It was as if he deliberately set
out to murder my mother. The man behaved like an
irresponsible animal. My poor mother. Why did she not
refuse him? Why did she not go to yourself or the
doctor? He knew it was likely to kill her. I refuse to
think anymore about it. It does something to me inside.

I am going to try to forget and as you said in your
letter let us have no more of this particular subject but
look forward to the brighter days ahead.

I think I mentioned in my last letter that we are producing a play for presentation some time after Christmas. Traditionally when there were female parts in a play the producer would inveigle gullible first year students to fill the roles. These were known as Starlets but they never quite measured up. Fortunately two of the three girl students are taking part this time. Both have already taken their degrees at National but are here doing a year's course in Theology.

Rehearsals are enjoyable. The play we are doing is 'Death of a Salesman' and I am playing the part of Willie Lomax. Make-up will be quite a problem. I must age thirty years if I am to be convincing. One of the girls, Jean Raymond, plays the part of my wife. She was born only twenty miles from Lochnanane in a place called Fahabawn. It appears that you were a curate there for a while during the never-to-be-forgotten reign of Father Donal 'Dynamite' Carey. When I get home for Christmas you must tell me all about him. He must have been a fantastic character. Take care of yourself and try not to expose yourself to the bad weather.

Write soon. Tell Mary Teresa I may have another tip very soon.

> Your affectionate nephew,
> Joseph.

※ ※ ※ ※ ※ • • • • • •

> The Presbytery,
> Lochnanane.

Dear Dring,

I am very much afraid you have landed yourself in serious trouble and it could well be that it was a black moment when the thought of visiting Trawbofin entered your head. Trawbofin, or in its translation into English, The Strand of the White Cow, is four miles from Lochnanane. The city of Cork is seventy-two miles from Lochnanane. On the day you presume to have seen Thomas Cooley on the strand of Trawbofin he was seventy-six miles away in the city of Cork on business. His brother Walter who teaches in Cork met him on his arrival and was with him in that ancient city by the Lee for a period of three hours. They spent the time in pubs and it is a known fact that the barmen in the public houses in Cork have most reliable memories.

Thomas Cooley left the city of Cork at seven o'clock in the evening. If it took him two hours to make the journey to Lochnanane it would have been dark on his arrival. As things turned out it was dark when he arrived at his mother's house on the evening in question.

His mother brought eleven children into this world of Drings and other things that go bump on the beach. She assures me that it was dark when he arrived. It is barely possible that you saw somebody who outwardly resembled Thomas Cooley that fateful evening (fateful for you). Mr. Cooley informs me that on a few occasions recently he has been seen at places where he could not possibly have been at the time. He informs me that there is an insurance agent in Castlepellick who is very like him in appearance, a chap of low morals who spent some time in England and who consorts with girls of doubtful reputation so that it could not possibly have been our friend who works in the chemist's shop and who is a veritable paragon by all accounts.

The gravity of your accusation is enormous now that it has been conclusively proved that you never saw Tom Cooley on the day you said you did and at the place you said you did and in the company of whom you said you did and in the state of undress you claim you saw them disport themselves.

You have put your two feet in it and all that remains for us to determine at this stage is if you told any others apart from myself. Better a millstone were tied around your neck, etc.

Tom Cooley is not a man for law but he will go to the supreme court if necessary. When I spoke to him he told me he would sue you for every penny you possess. He was shocked beyond belief when he heard the charge against him.

Knowing him to be a reasonable man I asked him

if he would consider settling out of court. He told me that he really wanted no material gain if you were prepared to withdraw the charge and say no more about it. An apology naturally would be in order as well. Drop me a line as I hate having callers in November.

Sincerely,
Martin O'Mora, P.P.

≋ ₂ • ≋ ▪ ≋ • • • • •

The Willows,
Gurtacreen,
Lochnanane.

Dear Father O'Mora,

I must have been mistaken although, in truth, if I were in a courtroom I would feel justified in swearing that Thomas Cooley was the man I saw in the nude at Trawbofin. The insurance agent you speak of would want to be an identical twin to make me do otherwise. However, there seems to be overwhelming evidence against me. I do not accept it but I will go along with what you suggest. I have no choice. I am the victim of circumstances. You will find the apology enclosed. You will not hear from me again nor indeed would I ever dream of calling to see you about anything ever again.

Yours faithfully,
Henry Dring, M.A.

≋ • • • ≋ ≋ ▪ • • • •

The Presbytery,
Lochnanane.

Dear Joe,

All is well that ends well. Our friend Henry Dring has withdrawn his charge against Tom Cooley. He also sent a letter of apology. I doubt if he will bother us again. I could never stand these self-appointed moralists. Any-

17

how I told Tom that I wanted to see him at the Presbytery and he called. He had no inkling of what I wanted him for.

I sat him down and gave him a drink, poured one for myself and for openers asked him if he knew our friend Henry Dring. The drink nearly fell from his hand. He admitted being at Trawbofin but said it was the heat and that there was nothing more to it. He also insisted that the girl wore a flesh-coloured panties and covered her breasts with her hands but that Dring must not have noticed in his agitation.

So Tom Cooley was guilty as charged or almost guilty. What was I to do? I like Tom and I happen to know that the little girl who works at the chemist's shop is a decent type at heart. It was a hot Autumn evening. They had neglected to bring togs. They saw nothing wrong in it. Tom admitted that he passed the remark of which Dring accused him but assured me that he often said the same to other girls with no harm intended. He promised it would stop.

I had to ask myself which was the more important; satisfaction for Dring or the future of a nice lad like Tom Cooley and the utter ruination of a girl's character.

It was then we composed the letter which brought the apology from Dring. He himself had given me the clue. You remember he wrote that no power on earth could stop him from going to the Civic Guards. There surely, said I to myself, is some drop of the Uncle's blood in this man's veins. No power on earth would stop his uncle either when the late canon made up his mind about something, no power, that is, except money. The late canon would do anything for money. That is why I suggested to Henry that Tom Cooley would sue him for every penny he possessed.

Knowing the seed, breed and generation of Henry Dring I guessed that the thought of losing one penny would be sufficient to make him abandon his course and see the light. I judged my man's weakness to a nicety. The only thing I regret is that he saw fit in his reply to say that he would never trouble me again. I have done him no harm, nor have I ever done any man deliberate harm since the day I was ordained. He may need me yet. For this reason it was foolish of him to say that he was burning his boats. I enclose a tenner. Don't ever refuse money unless you are certain it comes from an evil source. If you want any more let me know by return. Did you hear any more from your father? Write and let me know all.

> Your affectionate uncle,
> Martin O'Mora, P.P.

. . . .

> c/o Mrs. Joseph Mellington,
> Castle Avenue,
> Lochnanane.

Dear Father O'Mora,

I would call to see you but I am ashamed of myself and I am afraid people would put two and two together. I am pregnant and the man who I allowed do this to me cannot marry me as he is married himself. I don't know where to turn or what to do. My father would beat me up if I told him. He would also want to know the name of the man and this would not be possible for me to tell as it would cause nothing but trouble to a whole family that do not deserve it. If I told my mother she would tell my father she is so much afraid of him.

You know my father yourself. He is nearly always drunk. What am I to do Father. I am in terrible despair and I have thought of the river. Please do not ask me who the man is as I cannot tell. Will you please help me. I have heard from a girl who is my best friend that you never turn a person away. Please don't turn me away. I have made my mistake and it will last me for a lifetime. If you fail me it will mean I must go to England or do something dreadful.

> Sincerely yours,
> Bridget Day.

. . . .

Dear Uncle Martin,
Many thanks for your letter and the tenner. My father
will be coming with Mrs. Garrett the second week in
December for two days only. I have told him I look
forward to seeing him. He said in a letter that he would
like to talk to you. It's purely a matter for yourself.
All goes well. It's only a few minutes to six a.m. but
a few of us are catching up on our correspondence so
we rose rather early. There goes the Vox Dei. You
heard that bell often enough yourself to know that it is
a summons that must be answered. Let me know about
my father. That tenner wasn't really wanted but I
appreciate it as I do all the kindnesses you have always
shown me since my mother died. I hope I shall be able
to repay you some day.

In haste,
Joe.

* * * * * * * * * *

The Presbytery,
Lochnanane.

Dear Bridget Day,
Put England from your head this instant minute. England
is ninety per cent pure Pagan and you have no business
there. I'll grant you there are a few Catholic institutions
there which would accommodate you but I fear for you
afterwards. Enclosed herewith you will find twenty
pounds and a letter to a good friend of mine, Mother
Amabilis of the Convent of the Winged Servants of
Saint Sonia in Clonleary. I am, today, writing to her.
I assure you that you will be well taken care of and
do not worry about your father or indeed about anyone.
Just do as I tell you and leave the rest in my hands.
You poor girl. You have suffered your share as it is.

20

Pack your bag this very evening. The twenty pounds will help you buy any knick-knacks you may need. Follow carefully. Be at the main gate of my church at seven thirty on Friday morning. Father Raymond Tubridy, the parish priest of Lockeen, will be waiting for you. You know him by sight. He is the tall, red-haired man with the cross face. He will drive you direct to Clonlea. It's two hundred miles away and you can have your baby in peace and comfort when the time comes. I will look after everything else. I will write to you from time to time. Want for nothing. Be sure to write regularly and let me know your needs. Do not think you are without friends. The Virgin Mary will befriend you as she did so many others. Pray regularly and say one for me sometime.

Your Parish Priest and friend in J.C.
Martin O'Mora.

. . . .

Loafer's Lane,
Lochnanane.

Dear Father O'Mora,
I am no great spelerr. The agonys of the damd has me presued since the day I married the Monster. That's what we calls him now myself and the kids. He won't do a stroke of work and but for the family alounce we would starve. I am the mother of fourteen childeren and there is five more went to heaven. I have to work six days out of the seven and keep one of the older childeren inside from school. He stands all day with his back to the corner in the village woching the cars pasing and scraching himsef. You would nevver think wit his inocent face he was the same man woke this morning with a weapon would beat a ass out of a feld. He wanted his chips on the spot. I ran from the bed into the kichen an he arter me shoutin stand stand for me, steady you bludy bich. I had to go in the road in

case he knoc me up agin. I culd not have no more not if you gev me a millon. My helth wuld not stand it.

Culd it be cut of him some way. I stayed in the rode in the cold a hole hour and he roaring come in you effin skiv for the rich. The childeren wok for school so he went back to bed.

Save me from the monster, Father O'Mora. All people says you have a grate hart. Keep this sex manac off me no wuld I enjy one sumer wit a slack belly.

Your fateful servaent,
Rosie Monsey.

. . . .

Convent of the Winged Servants of St. Sonia, Clonleary.

Dear Martin,
Just arrived. Our little friend is in good hands. She has gone to watch television with another girl. I'll stay on a few days. I'm tired after the journey, a good deal more tired than I thought I would be. What can you expect at sixty four. I felt very honoured to be able to help Bridget. What a charming little girl she is. You know what she said to me when we were having lunch in Ballinasloe. 'Father,' said she, 'you're not cross at all. You're very nice.'

Good God, I never felt so complimented. It occurred to me more than once that the father of her child would be the head of the house where she worked. Maybe I'm wrong but we both know him well enough to know it is most likely. If it were a normal boyfriend she would name him. Why shouldn't she try to get a father for her child. Who would blame her. It has to be our friend. How many has he already in his own family? Five or six?

I played golf with him a month ago. You could not meet a more likeable fellow. Every man has his cross and he has his but I feel, Martin, that he should be

22

made to do something for Bridget. He must not be let off scot free. No better man than yourself to figure it out.

I haven't been well lately. I haven't told anybody but yourself. It may be the heart. Goodness knows the pains are bad enough across the chest. I'll see a doctor when I get home. Not to worry. Our friend is fine, thanks be to God. I'll call on my way home and you had better have a few bottles in. What's your new curate like?

Yours in J.C.
Ray.

* * * * * * * * * *

The Presbytery,
Lochnanane.

Dear Joe,

The Vox Dei Bell. I was often drugged in the deepest sleep when it roused me. I swear, that for us students, it made the Bells of Shandon sound like the rattle of an aluminium Rosary Beads. I will not see your father. I have forgiven him long since but I cannot be expected to condone his alliance with Mrs. Garrett. If I spoke to him I would be doing just that. He has betrayed his Catholic Faith deliberately. God knows we are all weak but God gave us the gifts of life and faith to cherish till we expire and I would be betraying my most cherished beliefs were I to speak to a man who married in a registry office. I'll say no more. You asked about Father Dan (Dynamite) Carey. God grant him a special place in heaven. He spent some years in America, before being appointed to the parish of Fahabawn. He brought two things from America. One was a heart of gold and the other an insatiable appetite for whiskey. The latter killed him. I was his first curate and I can say without fear of contradiction that Father Donal Carey was the finest priest and the decentest human being I have ever known. There is a story told about him that when he dropped dead in Killarney all that was found in his pockets was a corkscrew. This is true.

You may wonder why he was called Dynamite? Simple. He would often say to me when he would come in from a sick call: Martin, my ole buddy, pour me a shot of the goddam dynamite.

The dynamite was his undoing. He gave me my first car as a gift. When your mother died he found three hundred pounds somewhere for specialists. The people loved him. They would do anything for him. In all his time in Fahabawn, although he drank all round him, his name was never associated with drink. Woe betide the man who would dare to put a hard word on him. He died penniless. He had no possession of any kind except of course the corkscrew and the grace of God. It was he coined that immortal phrase about Ballybunion-by-the-sea. 'Ballybunion,' said he, 'where parish priests pretend to be sober and bank clerks pretend to be drunk.' I'll say no more for now. I have too much respect for his memory and I would only laugh out loud were I to recall his deeds. It was Dynamite who told me that every month the late Canon Dring would give a bundle of old newspapers to his altar boys with instructions that they be cut into pieces of a specified size. The pieces were used in the toilet. Apparently he would count them every day to ensure that nobody else was using the toilet. For the moment, farewell.

Your affectionate uncle,
Martin O'Mora, P.P.

•   ▪   •   •   ◂   •   •   •   •   •   •   •

Loafer's Lane,
Lochnanane.

Aha if twas the rich youd have them ansered long go. How is it not the poor. The keeping down of the poor is the wurk of the priests thes days I see for sure. The Monster struk agin las night an I sleeping. The docter

said the las time it was tech and go. I'm lucky I'm not
in the famly way. It wasent my time. His polci is strike
first and ask qestens arter. Will you cum to my aid or
I'll get the brednife to him soon. They shuld be cut off
all the men. I will rite to the bishop.

Your fateful servant,
Rosie Monsey.

■ ◄ • • • • ■ • • • •

The Presbytery,
Lochnanane.

Dear Mrs. Monsey,
I'm genuinely sorry for not answering your letter. What
you say is probably true. If it was a rich person I would
sit up and take notice at once. Forgive me and thank
you for telling me the truth. I will speak to your husband very soon. If you would tell him I need him for
some odd job I'm sure he would call. Meanwhile mind
yourself as best you can.

Yours in J.C.,
Your friend and P.P.,
Martin O'Mora.

• • • • • • • • • • •

The Presbytery,
Lochnanane.

Dear Ray,
A thousand thanks for driving our little friend to Clonleary. I would not have asked you had I known you
weren't feeling well. I'm glad you're going to see a
doctor. I'm sure all you need is a good, long rest. Stay
in Clonleary as long as you can. That's a great curate
you have. About my own. He began like a new broom

but as time passed the fibres lost their bristle and rigidity. He does not like work. He likes the company of women. I am all for being friends with women so long as there is no discrimination but the type he prefers is the young married one or the unpredictable nubile sort. He is never available to talk to older women. Any time I see him publicly at functions or in the street he is either giggling or whispering with some empty-headed girl. It has come to such a pass that I'm afraid I'll have to take him aside and talk to him.

I have received a few pointed anonymous letters. His liaisons with these feather-brains are quite harmless. He favours none openly as far as I know and this is good because there is safety in numbers. Inevitably the bishop, who has the cuteness of a pet fox and the long distance eye of a starving gannet, is bound to hop a ball. I can see him now scratching his chin before saying: 'Father, your curate would seem to be a great boon to the ladies,' then the pulling of the earlobe. 'Father, let us see what he can do for the ladies of the southwest.'

By the southwest, of course, he would mean the remotest outpost he could find. All very fine but new curates are getting scarcer and scarcer. It will have to be a talk.

I considered very carefully what you wrote in connection with the father of our little friend's expectation and there was no doubt in my mind but that you were on to the right man. I discovered from Sister Daphne of the Presentation Convent here in Lochnanane that Bridget Day passed her leaving certificate with two honours but failed to get a decent job. She took up temporary work with Mrs. Mellington, something to pass the time and earn a few quid while she waited for a break. Bridget's father is a bully and a drunkard. Her mother is a weakling, although not by choice.

Sister Daphne knows nothing about Bridget's trouble. I carefully covered all tracks, inventing a story here, planting a hint there with the result that everybody now believes Bridget Day stole away quietly to study nursing in England.

In view of what you said I decided to approach Mr.

Joseph Mellington. Easier said than done since I wanted the climate for our conversation to be nothing less than ideal on account of the subtleties involved. I thought of a number. I haven't caught a consistent club in five years but I remembered that when I was in my heyday it was Joe Mellington's burning ambition, and many another patsy, to beat me over eighteen holes. They never came remotely near it and they greatly supplemented my income when I was a curate in various pauperised places. I gave Joe a buzz and asked him for a game some morning when he would be free.

We were on the phone together at nine a.m. and we were on the links at ten. He knew I was rusty and he wanted quick vengeance. I played better than I thought I would but he had a shot over me to the sixteenth. The bet was a tenner and, all things allowed, I was prepared to lose if it would advance my cause. On our way to the seventeenth we stalled for a smoke. I always find when I am trying to get my pipe started is an ideal time to shoot a pertinent question.

'How's Irene?' I asked innocently.

'Fine, fine,' he said, 'never better.'

I expressed my delight and enquired after the children. They were in excellent form as was he and all connected with him. I said no more till after the seventeenth which we halved.

'God knows,' said I, 'you're a great man entirely the fine family and the fine happy home you have and the great business you built.'

This buoyed him up no end and he approached the eighteenth with confidence. I might have beaten him but I knew if he lost my case would be a hopeless one. He won by a stroke and I handed over the tenner. We strolled back to the clubhouse for a drink before lunch. I dawdled and began to frame my next question. Circumstantial evidence never hanged a man and that was all I had anyway you looked at it.

'Did Irene succeed in getting a new girl?' I asked.

'Who told you that she was looking for a new girl?'

'Ah I heard it just by chance. It could have been my housekeeper Mary Teresa. You know the way women are when one of them is looking for a girl. Word spreads.'

'She hasn't got one yet,' Joe Mellington said. 'Do you know of someone?'

I told him I didn't but that I would be on the look-out, that we often heard of girls looking for work.

'Where did the last girl go?' I asked. 'What's her name? Bridget Day wasn't it?'

'Yes,' he said, 'that was her name. She went to England to study nursing. I told her myself that she would be better off although I knew it would be hard to replace her.'

This convinced me that he was the man and from the way he spoke that he was a very relieved man. Without having to exert himself in the least he had disposed of a most serious problem. That he had dismissed the matter completely from his mind was also evident. I lost pity for him at this stage.

'Well, Joe,' I said, 'Bridget Day is not gone to England to study nursing and you did not tell her that she would be better off if she were to do so. She could not do so, Joe, for the simple reason that she is expecting a baby and that baby, please God, will be delivered in this country.'

He was flabbergasted but, by God, he came round like a shot. He wouldn't have got to where he is if he wasn't tough. I waited a minute before I delivered the next one. 'Why did you say you advised her to go nursing when we both know you didn't.'

'I did tell her,' he said.

'I have her word,' I told him, 'that you did not and whatever else that little girl may be. she is not a liar.'

To this he made no immediate reply. He may have won the curtain raiser but I was winning the main bout.

'Maybe I did. Maybe I didn't,' he said.

'Alright,' I said, 'but let me tell you a few interesting facts, Joe. I happen to know that the father of the child is a married man with a family. I happen to know that he is a native of Lochnanane and the reason that Bridget Day refused to expose him was because she was afraid of the effect it would have on that man's wife and children.'

'Was this what you brought me out here for?' he asked, 'to tell me this?'

I admitted that it was.

'Are you implying that I might be the father of the child?'

'Joe,' I said, 'one of my parishioners is in trouble. I have no desire to see two of you in trouble.'

'Is that supposed to be a threat?' he asked, 'because if it is you're talking to the wrong man. I take threats from nobody. I am my own man.'

'Joe,' I said, 'don't come the heavy with me. You are the man responsible for Bridget Day's misfortune,' I shouted, 'now what are you going to do about it?'

'For God's sake,' he begged, 'keep your voice down. Do you want the whole country to hear?'

'What are you going to do about it?' I shouted.

He begged me not to raise my voice. I told him I would lower it when he told me what he planned to do for Bridget Day.

'What do you want me to do?' He was a changed man. The fear showed in his voice.

'I want her to have a university education,' I told him, 'and I want you to pay for it.'

'You're mad,' he said.

'Give me a thousand pounds,' I told him, 'and I'll see that she gets that education when her troubles are over.'

He told me he could not lay his hands on that kind of money.

'This is a girl,' I said, 'who may well want to keep her child. She must have the means to support it. She must be independent. You owe it to her.'

'A thousand is ridiculous,' he said. 'I haven't got it.'

'Joe,' I said, 'you drive a three thousand pound plus car. You recently bought two farms. You are the biggest contractor in these parts. My patience is coming to an end. I'm really doing you a favour.'

'It's blackmail,' he said. I told him I did not like the word blackmail, that it was unfair, that justice was the word. 'You'll have my cheque tomorrow, Father,' he said meekly.

You can tell Bridget the news. Don't say where the money came from. Tell her it's a private fund long since created to help girls in distress who have this capacity for university education. The money will be in the form of a trust. You, Bridget and I will administer. I got a present of a turkey from a friend. Let me know the day you are coming home and we'll try the bird out.

Your friend,
Martin.

•   •   •   •   •   •   •   •   •   •   •

St. Unshin's,
Ballyrango.

Dear Uncle Martin,

Many thanks for your letter. I had guessed that you would not see my father. Enough said. All goes well here with the production of the play moving smoothly. The elocution classes are an immense asset especially if a person wants to act. I loved your stories about Dynamite and Canon Dring. Any more? It can be very dull here in November. Did you plant any more daffodils? How is Mary Teresa? Tell her she is very slow about answering my letter. How about the new curate? What's he like? I want to know all.

Affectionately,
Joe.

•   •   •   •   •   •   •   •   •   •

Loafer's Lane,
Lochnanane.

Dear Father O'Mora,

Hel be doun to see you Fridey. He compland of a pain in the back when I sed you wantd him but hel be doun

Fridey for sure. Oh chastis him the low hound that give me no peace. Im dead if i have another child. Chastis the monster get him operate on by some surgin. Whip the fako off him. Don't say i sed nothing whatever you do.

Your fateful servant,
Rosie Monsey.

.   .   .   .

The Presbytery,
Lochnanane.

Dear Joe,

All goes well. Glad you enjoyed the stories about Dyna-mite and Dring. There are still some great characters in the diocese. I refuse to answer any questions about my new curate beyond saying that he is opposed to work. He doesn't like it and he is never around when he's wanted. He would want to catch on to himself. Mary Teresa is fine. She is a great housekeeper in all respects, unique in fact.

She always minds her own business yet she knows enough to run the parish in case of emergency. I planted another hundred of daffodil bulbs and a score of copper beeches, ten at either side of the presbytery. If my pre-decessor, the late Father John Clement Fitzraymond had planted in his time we would have trees now. I still get his bills. I honour them. They are mostly for intoxi-cating drink and tinned delicacies such as crab, lobster etc. The parish clerk was once examining empty bottles to see if there was anything left when Fitzy popped out of nowhere.

'They are all dead you fool,' said he.

'Thank God they didn't die without a priest,' said the clerk.

Another time the parish clerk was chasing ducks out of the presbytery kitchen.

'Go on. Shag off outa that,' he was saying when he was surprised by Fitzy.

'Listen,' said Fitzy. 'You shouldn't tell those ducks shag off. Never use rotten language in front of ducks. Just say cush, cush and they'll shag off themselves.'

You heard me say often enough that Canon Dring was the second meanest priest in the diocese. It's time I told you who the meanest one was. He was Father Tom Winder of Tubberdarrig. His first curate was a meek man called James Dee. On the occasion of their first breakfast together the housekeeper delivered one boiled egg to Father Tom Winder but nothing to Father Dee.

Dee waited expectantly for some addition to his meagre allotment of one slice of bread but he waited in vain.

'Do you like eggs, Father?' asked Winder.

'I love 'em,' said the curate.

'So do I,' said Winder. With that he took the cap off the egg and placed it in front of Dee.

'There is more nourishment in the cap of one hen-egg,' said Winder, 'than there is in a pound of meat.' After that Father Jim Dee ate out whenever possible. One of our late lamented bishops was once dined by Father Winder. There was buttered bread and roast beef. The bishop lifted a slice of bread and examined it.

'The man that buttered this bread,' said his Lordship, 'would grease the road from here to Dublin with one pound of butter.'

'Have you anything to say about the beef?' said Father Dee hopefully.

The bishop lifted a slice of beef.

'Can you see through your like I can through mine?' asked Dee.

'I can,' said the bishop. 'With a roast cut as thinly as this I could cover the walls of every bedroom in my palace.'

The only effect that this unkindly banter had on Winder was that he released a huge guffaw and slapped the bishop on the back.

'You're a gay and airy man my Lord,' said he. 'May the good God leave you gay and airy for many a day to come.'

You may wonder Joe about the hardness of my attitude towards your father. He married outside his Faith which means he turned his back on a true authority. For a man of his age and education to do this was irresponsible. Authority is what holds the world together. I accept the Pope as the be-all and end-all in authority. There are no deviations on my part from this complete acceptance. It is natural for me and nature is not easily checked. Your father failed when he ceased to accept the teachings of the Catholic Church. He thereby turned his back on the real meaning of authority, of respect for and maintenance of it. Without authority there can be no order. Without authority all things must fall asunder inevitably. Without authority there can be no love or no peace. Abandon authority and you invite anarchy to your dominions. That is why I utterly reject and utterly detest anything which is opposed to authority. Authority is God.

If I seem adamantine about the Catholic Faith in regard to your father it is out of respect for authority. You see about you today what this lack of respect is leading to. In a sense the Pope is my father. I obey him and accept him as a child accepts the dictates of its parents. To defy the Pope is to destroy the meaning of authority with its attendant virtues such as the idea of peaceful co-existence, the idea of a true and lasting love, the rearing of a family, in fact all the virtues.

Those who oppose the laws of the Catholic Church oppose authority. In their youth or ignorance or plain fecklessness there are many priests and people who question the Pope's authority. They question his infallibility. They question traditions. What they are doing, whether they are aware of it or not, is rebelling childishly against authority because they find the necessary strictures of the Church too binding.

In or out of the Church these types will wreck community effort and order. They may be right in part. So what? We are all right in part even when we differ. None of our ideas are identical no more than our faces and bodies are, but there are no two ways if you are a member of the Catholic Church. It is the first and last authority. It is universal. Remember too that if I ever seem unbending in matters of Canon Law that I was suckled on the Code.

To return to Father Tom Winder. He lived to be ninety-two and in so doing survived most of his curates. Some day, some far-seeing curate or P.P., who knew him better than I, will do a book on him. 'He was so mean,' said poor Jimmy Dee, 'that if he was a ghost he wouldn't give you a fright.'

Here is what his housekeeper said about him: 'He was that perished,' said she, 'that he'd begrudge you the steam of his water.' Once during a confirmation breakfast he made eleven sandwiches out of two ounces of ham. That's one for the Guinness Book of Records. His parish clerk Dickie Molyneaux looked like Uriah Heap. He was paid a pittance and even the station money he received had to be divided with Winder. Dickie carried the altar wine around in a Baby Power bottle which he kept in his waistcoat pocket. He would produce the bottle during the Offertory. There was no bell but Dickie had iron tips on the heels of his boots and he would click those heels together whenever necessary. The sound was as good as that produced by a bell. The congregation took it for granted.

You may ask what Winder did with his money. No one ever found out. He disliked bishops and once when he saw several together was heard to remark: 'Will you look at the corpulent wretches strutting among the novices like drunken colonels in the Mexican army.'

Even when he was a curate he was mean. He once got a present of a case of Scotch. First of all he tried to sell it but he was so unpopular that he could get nobody to buy it off him.

He locked it in his chest. Every curate had a chest in those days. The housekeeper had a notorious tooth for the hot stuff and because of this Winder kept a close eye on the chest. As close as he watched it the whiskey began to disappear. Rightly or wrongly he suspected the housekeeper. What did he do but put a rabbit trap on top of the whiskey case. He cleverly fixed the chest so that it could only be partly opened. In other words whoever rifled inside would not see the trap until it was too late. He then told the housekeeper that he would be gone for the day. The day passed and when he arrived home it was dark. The housekeeper was sitting on a chair by the fire in the kitchen. Her hand was bandaged.

'Wisha what happened you girl?' he declared full of mock sympathy.

'Kiss me arse,' she said and no more. He was a hard and a merciless man.

When Father Dee first came to Winder he had a horse which he rode to his sick calls. When he went on a fortnight's holiday Winder did not give the horse a solitary sop of hay, blade of grass or grain of oats. The horse was hardly able to stand when Father Dee returned from his holiday.

At once the curate fed the poor animal with a large bucket of oats. Then he brought the horse indoors. Inside he led the animal around Winder's study several times until it had fully discharged itself.

I could go on all day but I have to hear confessions. Take care of yourself and write soon.

Your affectionate Uncle,
Martin O'Mora, P.P.

. . . .

Loafer's Lane,
Lochnanane.

Dear Father O'Mora,
The Monster is a lamb. He havint come near me since. You mus hav give him a grate talking to. He don't try cum aroun me no more. You mus hav pourin the blessed water on his fako. He still doun at the corner scratchin hisself and countin the cars passin. What the cars do if he not there.

Your fateful servant,
Rosie Monsey.

. . . .

Dear Ray,

There is a character here called Jack Monsey who is
nicknamed the Monster by his unfortunate wife. She
has babies year in, year out and often every ten months.
Apart from this Jack does nothing except to hold up
the village corner from morning till night.

For weeks now she has been pestering me to talk to
Jack. Anyhow I got him into the Presbytery on the
grounds that I had some odd jobs for him. I have no
doubt whatever but that Rosie Monsey would die if she
was to have another baby. Jack Monsey is an ignorant
man and you will agree that if you want to get anywhere with ignorance, ritual is the answer.

I put a white smock on Mocky Dolan the parish
clerk and held him in readiness while I interviewed Jack
in the sitting room. First I put Jack sitting down and
then I looked out the sitting room window for a full
ten minutes. You could almost hear the sweat oozing
from his pores.

'Jack,' I said, 'it is my painful duty to inform you
that the Jesuits are on to you.' I let this sink in and
watched his face turn ashen grey.

'What did I do?' he asked.

'Something terrible indeed,' I told him, 'because the
Jesuits never bother ordinary sinners.'

'Is there no hope for me?' he asked with a crack in
his voice and the tears beginning to show in his eyes.

'Don't despair,' I advised him.

'There is a hope for every consostasite who is prepared to recant although in your case the situation may
have gone too far. First of all you must give me your
sacred word that you will refrain from having intercourse with your wife.'

'I never done that,' said he. 'I never stooped to that.'

'Jack,' I explained, 'intercourse means mounting your
wife.' He nodded solemnly.

'You must give me your most sacred word that it

will stop until such time as she can have no more babies. Nothing less than your sacred word will do.'

'Will you call the Jesuits off me if I do?' At this stage he was bawling.

'That I cannot promise,' I said, 'until the following obligations are fulfilled.' Again he nodded solemnly.

'First,' I told him, 'you must be resuminated and properly contracted. You must also be filtrated and fumigated and in order to do these things properly the bishop will have to be written to for a loan of vestments and the college of cardinals contacted for oil of olives.'

'Good God,' Jack cried out as he crossed himself. 'Help me Father,' he begged. It was precisely at this moment that I called in the parish clerk. He was well rehearsed. He liberally sprinkled Jack with holy water (which will do him no harm anyhow) and muttered some mumbo-jumbo under his breath. Jack was impressed. The parish clerk walked round him till he had made three full circles. He sprinkled him with more holy water and walked round him a second time till three more full circles were completed. Then the parish clerk withdrew walking slowly backwards, head bent, still muttering for all he was worth.

'Stand up,' I ordered Jack. He leaped to his feet. By this time he was trembling like a leaf but I reminded myself that watching a trembling ignoramus was better than looking at the mother of fourteen laid out on a slab.

'Jack Monsey,' I addressed him in a stentorian tone. 'You have now been made ready for consalmination.' He nodded eagerly.

'Do you promise,' I asked him, 'never to touch your wife's body until the doctor says it is safe to do so?'

'I promise,' he said. 'I promise. I promise. I promise.'

'Alright,' I told him, 'I will see what can be done for you. The final word will rest with Rome but be assured that the Bishops of Ireland will not be dumb when your case comes up.'

He clutched my hands in his and went on his knees thanking me. I sent him on his way. I had a letter from his wife a short time ago to thank me for what I had done for her. Apparently he has left her alone since.

Only yesterday I sent Mary Teresa to fetch Rosie Monsey to the presbytery. We gave her a cup of tea and made her feel at ease. The poor woman never had a day off in her life apart from her confinements which never lasted more than two days believe it or not. One for Ripley surely.

We discovered that she has a sister married to a soldier in Cork. The sister's husband is a decent sort of man and on numerous occasions they asked her to the city for a few days. Between one thing and another she never got there. She once managed to put aside six pounds but the Monster found it and spent it on drink.

While the Monster is still recovering from the shock of our interview and conducting himself in an exceptional fashion by his standards we have decided to send her off to Cork to the sister. Her oldest girl can manage the house. I gave her enough money for a decent holiday and enough to buy some new clothes. The poor woman was overcome. Ray would you believe it when I tell you that never once in her twenty years of marriage did she or one of her children eat a plate of rashers and eggs in that house. I may tell you that they will eat them from now on and I will personally see to it that she has a holiday every year. I do not want you volunteering to drive her to Cork, let her go by bus. It will be a bigger treat for her. My curate is gone to the dogs. He has women on the brain. He spends all day and all night chasing them. It looks as if I'll have to chat him up. Speaking about dogs. I was once a curate with Father Dick Hobbs. Dick, as you know, was a great man for the greyhounds.

He could never be found for parish duties when the track season started. The result was that the letters began to pour in to the bishop from well-meaning souls in the parish.

One day his Lordship arrived and took Dick aside.

'Dick,' he said, 'you know me. The last thing I want to do is interfere with the running of the parish but Dick you are rocking the boat.'

'In what way would I be rocking the boat my Lord?' said Dick innocently.

'I have it on good authority that you are more interested in greyhounds than in your parishioners,' said the bishop.

'There may be a grain of truth in that,' answered Dick, 'but my Lord it is not by choice. I am addled with thoughts of beautiful women. It is a terrible cross but I find that my interest in greyhounds negatives my interest in women.'

'Is that a fact?' said the bishop and he pulled his left earlobe.

'As God is my judge,' said Dick.

'Look,' said the bishop, 'don't worry any more about my visit. Try to train your dogs without attracting too much attention and everything will be alright.' With that the bishop departed and Dick trained his dogs with his head in the air from then on. A month later he had an urgent letter from the bishop requesting a greyhound pup.

As ever,
Martin.

.   .   .   .

St. Unshin's College,
Ballyrango.

Dear Uncle Martin,

There is little news from this place except that the play goes well and that I am progressing with my studies. I love your stories. Was there ever a book of clerical anecdotes gathered from round the diocese. I'd love to do it some time. I might even get an M.A. for it. I'm not serious of course but it has the germ of a good idea. I daresay the bishop's approval would be needed.

Last week we had a guest producer for a few days. This man has a very original approach. Afterwards he spoke to us about the modern theatre and modern poetry. He made a scathing attack on the likes of

Shelley and Keats and said that their work was childish and idiotically romantic. Jean disagreed with him but he made some novel points.

How is Mary Teresa? That tip failed to materialise but there should be others. Take care of yourself. I look forward to Christmas. I need your advice on a few matters.

Affectionately,
Joe.

* * • • • * * • • • •

Randle's Terrace,
Cork.

Dear Father O'Mora,

Just a line to let you know Im having a marvless time here with pitchers every night and holy mass in the morning. We go an we have chips after the pitchers and they are luvey. I pray for you. Its a luvey time.

Your fateful servant,
Rosie Monsey.

* * • • • • • • • • •

St. Philomena's Nursing Home,
Lochnanane.

Dear Father O'Mora,

You will find no name signed at the end of this letter but please do not ignore it. Every word I say is true but I dare not become involved. I am one of the staff here and I hope you will keep it a secret that you were put wise by one of the staff. This is very important to me.

One night last week a girl from the parish was rushed in by Doctor Mick Moffy. It was all hush-hush and instead of being put into one of the wards she was taken to Mrs. Clavey's private quarters. About two hours later

she was taken to the labour ward and not too long afterwards a pair of twins was delivered. What makes me
suspicious is that all the babies were taken down to be
christened last Sunday at two o'clock but the twins were
not taken at all. The mother of the twins left yesterday
and it would seem that Doctor Claffy is now in control.
The mother has gone back to work as if nothing happened. I do not wish to stir up trouble but I hope I am
a good Catholic.

This summer I was in the lounge of a certain hotel
in a certain seaside resort and near me were Doctor
Moffy and his wife with two English visitors a husband
and wife as well. From the conversation I gathered that
he and Doctor Moffy had gone to the same university
in Galway and that he was an engineer. They had no
family and I think they had no religion unless maybe
they were some sort of Protestants. During the talk I
learned that the pair had no family and she made
Doctor Moffy promise he would be on the look-out for
a nice child with a good background to adopt.

'Maybe twins,' she said and she clapped her hands.

'Oh, I would love to adopt a pair of twins,' she said.
If you put two and two together Father you will see
what I mean. Are these twins destined for a non-
Catholic home in England and who gives Doctor Moffy
the right to hand them over.

I think this is a case where you should stop at nothing
to save these Catholic infants from a faith worse than
death.

Sincerely,
One who tries to be a
good Catholic.

■　　●　　●　　●　　●　　▪　　●　　●　　●　　●　　●

The Presbytery,
Lochnanane.

Dear Joe,
Great to hear from you and glad that the studies and
the play go well. November is a lonely time everywhere

in the Catholic world. We are remembering our dead. It is a month of mourning. I am amused by this new producer especially since he knocks Shelley who was a great friend to Irish Catholics in a time when friends were few. The first verse of the only decent poem I ever learned in the seminary at the age of thirteen was from Shelley's Cloud:

I bring fresh showers for the thirsting flowers,
From the seas and the streams;
I bear light shade for the leaves when laid
In their noonday dreams.
From my wings are shaken the dews that waken
The sweet buds every one
When rocked to rest on their mother's breast
As she dances about the sun.
I wield the flail of the lashing hail
And whiten the green plains under
And then again I dissolve it in rain
And laugh as I pass in thunder.

Ah well. Maybe that producer knows more than I do. I look forward to Christmas too and to seeing you. I'll be glad to give you any advice you want although, quite honestly Joe, you always struck me as a man who needed no advice from anybody. Speaking about advice I am reminded of the advice the tinker gave to his son:

'Mount away,' said he, 'but marry at home.'

'Be sure,' said he, 'always to stand your horse in the middle of the fair and to always take the morning price.'

'Never go between a husband and wife for that is to go between the bark and the tree. Most of all be sure to test your friend before you need him.'

The tinker hadn't much else to give but maybe what he gave was better than money. I like the last piece. Test your friend before you need him. It's worth remembering.

Joe I'll tell you something. When I was at the stage where you are at now I had problems, serious problems. I went to friends for advice but they had none to give. It is a tough and trying time with your subdeaconate coming up and celibacy to boot. Anyhow write and let me know what's troubling you, why wait till Christmas?

Your affectionate Uncle,
Martin O'Mora, P.P.

. . . .

The Presbytery,
Lochnanane.

Dear Doctor Moffy,
I have come from Saint Philomena's Nursing Home where I have had a long and profitable chat with the proprietress, Mrs. Clavey. I have given instructions that those twins be baptised on Wednesday next. I'll countenance no objection. I have also been to the mother of the twins and I have got her to agree to sign a document transferring the twins to my care i.e. to a Catholic Orphanage of my choosing where they will remain until they are adopted by worthy Catholic parents. I would hereby ask you to refrain from visiting the twins again.

Yours in J.C.
Father Martin O'Mora.

. . . .

The Dispensary,
Lochnanane.

Dear Father O'Mora,
I would like to remind you that we are not living in the middle ages when a superstitious and benighted peasantry believed that priests could turn them into goats. Your letter is a monstrous insult to my profession and to my personal integrity. Here is the full story of what happened.
One night last week I was called by the girl's mother to her home. She told me she feared that her daughter

43

had an appendix and that she should have it out. Poor innocent woman.

I went upstairs to examine the girl and discovered that the appendix pains were not appendix pains at all. They were labour pains. I came downstairs and reported my findings to the mother whose only reaction was to scream selfishly and invoke the aid of that greatly over-worked trio Jesus, Mary and Joseph. In an inkling she calmed down. 'She can't have it here,' she shouted, 'she can't have it here. Her father would strangle her. Her brothers would crucify her. What would the neigh-bours say. Oh Jesus doctor get her out of here.'

I did as this fine Christian parent told me and took the girl to Saint Philomena's where in order to avoid publicity I placed the girl in Mrs. Clavey's private quarters. Shortly thereafter I delivered the twins. Those twins are my responsibility. The day after I delivered them into this world of dictatorial clergymen and cowardly parents I rang a friend of mine, a professional man with a fine home and a good job not to mention a lovely wife.

To fulfil a promise I made to him some time ago I told him that he could have the twins. His wife came on the phone and begged me not to allow them be baptised until she found sponsors and arranged for a christening in her own town.

After I received your letter I went to the mother of the twins. She was at home with her own mother. I asked both the mothers to remember that it was I who helped them in their hour of need, who saved a reputa-tion and arranged everything. They agreed that they owed more to me than to you.

The result was that I drew up a document declaring the note she gave to you to be manufactured under duress and that forthwith I was to be the sole and rightful guardian of the twins.

Sincerely yours,
Michael Moffy, M.B.

. . . .

Dear Ray,

After Moffy's last letter I decided there was no point in further writing so I went and bearded the scoundrel in his den. 'You are here,' he said pompously, 'after dispensary hours.'

'I am here on God's business,' I told him.

'What do you want?' he asked.

'I want,' said I, 'that you stop interfering with God's work and keep away from those twins.'

'The twins are in my care,' he bellowed like a bull.

'The twins are in my parish and let's see you try to take them out of it?' I told him.

'I can see you have been talking to people,' he said. 'What about the reputation of the mother?'

'Which is more important,' I asked him, 'the reputation of a girl who is a know maleficent or the souls of two innocents? Will you damn them forever by allowing them to be brought up in another faith or maybe no faith at all?'

He laughed at this.

'Christ Almighty,' he said, 'why don't you pop back into the nineteenth century and stay there this time? What difference does it make what religion they have as long as they are happy and content?'

'They will not be baptised Protestants,' I warned him.

'How do you know they won't be Hindus?' he scoffed.

'Listen doctor,' I reminded him, 'maybe you don't care whether they are Catholics or not but they might when they are old enough to know.'

'Fine,' he said, 'let's wait till they're twenty-one and we'll ask them what they want to be. Maybe they might like to be Quakers or Lutherans or Mormons or Presbyterians. If they have any sense they'll have nothing to do with any of you. Now I'm a busy man Father and I have important reports to make out.'

'Those twins,' I told him finally, 'were born of a Catholic mother in a Catholic Nursing Home. The laws

of God and State command that they be baptised
Catholics. Do not interfere further,' I warned him, 'or
you will bring the wrath of God and the full force of
the civil law on your head.' With that I slammed the
door on him and walked off.

                              I'll report further,
                              As ever,
                              Martin.

♦   •   •   •   ⸳   ⸳   •   •   •   •   •

                                   The Elms,
                                   Louchnanane.

Dear Father O'Mora,
I have never troubled you up to this but I feel that you
are the only one I can turn to. I am, as you probably
know, a spinster and I live in retirement here at the
Elms with my housekeeper Josephine Lalor.
    Recently a local drunkard, Sammy Seller has been
causing me some annoyance and embarrassment not to
mention the embarrassment he causes other people. I
cannot quite bring myself to tell you what it is wrong
but I suppose I had better begin somewhere.
    On his way home he persists in urinating at the en-
trance to the avenue leading to my house. He exposes
himself for long periods and even when the children are
on their way home from school or old ladies are passing he refuses to button himself. It is all dreadfully
embarrassing and I am afraid to go to the Guards in
case they might expect me to act as a witness to this
sordid and revolting business. You are the one person
I feel I can trust.
    The other evening he was there so long that my
housekeeper Josephine went down the avenue. I feel
I oughtn't tell you how she addressed him but it has to
be told.
    'Get out of here you tramp,' she screamed at him,

'and stop showing off your dirty oul' drumstick while you're urinating.'

'That's what it's for,' he called, back at her, 'for urinating. That's what I got it for. It helps get the water out.' What are we to do, Father? Please help us.

Sincerely yours,
Cliona O'Gairea.

＊ ● ● ● ● ● ● ● ● ● ● ●

The Presbytery,
Loughnanane.

Dear Joe,
How goes it? I have been fairly busy with important matters and that is the reason for the delay in writing. I won't trouble you with some recent happenings here except to tell you that that ruffian Sammy Seller has been up to his old tricks again. He must have been fined in the local court at least twenty times for indecent exposure or urinating in public places. I never interfered until the other evening. I got a report that he was piddling publicly above and beyond the call of duty at the gate leading to O'Gairea's old house just outside the village. I wrote to Miss O'Gairea and told her to give me a ring on the phone if he troubled her again.

The following evening the phone rang. It was Miss O'Gairea. She informed me that our friend Sammy was up to his old tricks. I hopped into the car and in a minute I was at the scene of the crime. There he was with one hand resting on the wall in front of him and the other holding his lightning rod. I did not wait to see whether he was piddling or showing off. I got out of the car and approached him noiselessly from behind. I had on my strong boots. When I found myself within range I drew back and I let him have a mighty kick in the posterior. He jumped five feet in the air.

'My bum is burst,' he cried out. I let him have a second dose of the boot on the same target. I am prepared to lay you odds that he will never expose himself publicly again.

I suppose you could say that it was just another incident in the daily routine of the parish. Reports about like happenings come in all the time. Once a week without fail there is a plea from some unfortunate wife to come and talk to her husband. It follows a pattern. There she is, at maybe three or four o'clock in the morning in her nightgown, huddled up with the cold against the doorway having been ejected for no reason by a drunken husband or maybe 'tis how the poor creature would have her bag packed to go home or if there was no home then anywhere so long as there would be a respite from the blackguarding she receives. It is the function of the priest to resolve these problems. There is nobody else to do it.

You have heard the expression, man's inhumanity to man, but believe me Joe there is nothing as awful as the inhumanity of husband to wife. Much of it may be the wife's fault and it is my task to find out where the blame lies and to apportion that blame fairly. Most couples want reconciliation desperately and it is a pleasure to steer them on a proper course. With others it is a waste of time. In nearly all cases it is the fault of the husband. Drink is a wonderful thing in moderation but drink in the belly of an inconsiderate or selfish husband means misery for his unfortunate wife. We Irish have many virtues and many faults. If I was asked to list our worst fault I would point a finger at the drunken husband.

Yesterday I planted twenty chestnut trees, ten at either end of the drive. When I'll be dead and gone some priest will remember me kindly, far kindlier than I remember Father John Clement Fitzraymond. He never planted a shrub not to mention a tree.

Here's one for your collection. When Canon Dring received his first parish he was visited by an old woman who told him that she wanted Mass said for her late husband.

'That will be a guinea, missus,' said Dring.

'I haven't any money, Canon,' said the old woman.

'High money for high mass,' said Dring, 'low money for low mass and no money for no mass.'

'But,' said the old woman, 'all the new priests oblige me by saying a free mass for him.'

'How long is he dead?', asked Dring.

'Thirty years, Canon,' said the old woman.

'Missus,' said Dring, 'a Mass won't make the slightest difference to him at this stage but that is not to say I would turn you away were you to come back with a guinea.'

My new curate is a pain.

'There will have to be a raise,' he announced at breakfast yesterday. There is a law which says a curate is entitled to eleven pounds ten shillings a year. The law was never repealed. According to this law he is entitled to free firing from the first of November to the first of April. He can keep mass offerings and he gets his cut (quite substantial) from the November offerings. At the stations he gets Petrol Money. This was known as Oats money when there were no motor cars. In short he gets plenty and if he works his loaf he can put himself in the way of many an offering. With the right approach he could treble his income.

'I am not obliged to give you a raise,' I informed him.

'Fair enough,' he said.

'Are you short of money?' I asked. 'I have been short of money since the day I came here,' he said.

'Don't be smart,' I told him, 'I know how much you're knocking down.'

'Look,' he said, 'I want a new car.'

'So do I,' I told him.

'I should have known what to expect,' he said.

'Listen here now my boy,' I started, 'I will take no lip from you. Is it how you think I don't know you're out till all hours chatting up dames? Is it how you think I wouldn't know the smell of stale brandy as good as the next man? I was a curate too remember. You would do well to change your tack,' I told him. I was about to continue when he rose from the table. 'You're as big a bore as Pope Paul,' he said, 'and that's some bore.'

That was his curtain line. He has been dining out

since, no doubt with those eejits of women in the upper crust here. I'll close now. Take care of yourself.

Your affectionate uncle,
Martin O'Mora, P.P.

* • • • • • • • • •

The Presbytery,
Lochnanane.

Dear Ray,

The drama of the Terrible Twins, as I will call it, is all over and I am sorry to have to say that victory went to Doctor Moffy. I'll start at the beginning. Last Saturday morning I got a call from Mrs. Clavey, proprietress of Saint Philomena's Nursing Home. She told me that Doctor Moffy had stolen the twins and was on his way to Shannon Airport, presumably to take them to England and place them in the hands of his Protestant fellow-conspirators.

I rounded up the curate and ordered him to ring every presbytery between here and Shannon. Then I went straight to the Guards' Barracks and notified them. There was an immediate alert. The local patrol car set out at once but broke down after three miles. The only patrol car available within a radius of thirty miles set off in hot pursuit but a puncture soon put an end to her daring bid. The spare was soft and there was no pump so she was rendered hors de combat too.

It was now up to the Church alone and the Church was not found wanting. Like chain reaction one parish notified its neighbour and the upshot was that there were a hundred pairs of eyes between Shannon and the village of Lochnanane on the look-out for the Doctor's Mercedes.

He never showed up on this route so I became suspicious. Was there a middleman. I had to wait till nightfall to discover the truth. Here is what happened. After absconding with the twins he changed cars a mile from Lochnanane. He transferred his little charges to the

50

other car and hit for Cork. You will have to agree that nobody knows the backroads better than a dispensary doctor. Anyhow he got away and handed over the children to a couple in Cork. The couple are Catholics, well thought-of and well-off. He might have told me that he wasn't handing them over to Protestants. He now wants an apology. I did what I thought best. He will get no apology from me. He is going around the pubs accusing me of bigotry. I have my sources. Here is what he said at one pub: 'O'Mora,' said he, 'is suffering from an overdose of racial memory aggravated by religious bigotry.'

Let him alone. He'll prove to be his own undoing one day. He'll never get an apology from me. Call when you get a chance.

As ever,
Martin.

. . . .

Church Street,
Lochnanane.

Dear Father O'Mora,
I don't know am I doing right or wrong in writing to you. God knows I have been on my knees long enough trying to come to a decision. The notion to let you know what's going on has me possessed this good bit but I decided that after what happened last night I would have to inform you.

Sometimes my line of work keeps me out late and I see things that I am not meant to see. I live a few doors from the house of Daisy Redlap in Church Street. A fortnight ago the piano was going in that house till half-past one in the morning. From half-eleven till one o'clock Miss Redlap herself did the singing but from one on she was joined by a male voice. He was a tenor, quite good and I was most anxious to find out who it was as I hadn't heard the voice in the Lochnanane Church Choir.

The night's entertainment ended with the song, 'Beautiful Dreamer.' After that there was silence for several minutes. Then I heard a door bang in the street so I tiptoed downstairs to see who was the owner of the excellent voice. As I opened the street door your curate Father Carrity was just passing by. There wasn't a sign of another Christian on the street. It must have been him that was doing the singing.

'Good-night, my child,' he said to me very sarcastic in tone.

'Good-night, Father,' said I, 'you're out very late.'

'A sick call,' he said gaily and went off towards the presbytery whistling. That was a fortnight ago. He has been at Redlap's every night since but last night crowned it. They sang till half-past four and as the night wore on the singing got worse. Very uneven and a trifle harsh. As soon as I heard the door bang I went downstairs for a breath of fresh air. Your curate was coming up the street taking the two sides of it. 'Good-night, Father,' I said, 'you're out very late again.'

'God's work,' he stammered and he nearly collapsed at my feet. I steered him towards the presbytery. I will say no more as I know you will take care of the matter. It is not for us to judge.

> Sincerely,
> One who tries to be a good Catholic.

P.S.: I'm past 40 and when I first went to Secondary school, Daisy Redlap was doing her leaving.

O.W.T.T.B.A.G.C.

. . . .

The Presbytery,
Lochnanane.

Dear Joe,

Enjoyed your letter. I am indeed glad that you hit it
off so well with your father. As I have told you so often
you must never allow my opinion of him to influence
you. I will be at Mallow to meet your train on Saturday
week. Eight days is a goodly spell and I look forward
to having you. I enclose twenty-five pounds in case you
decide to buy your Christmas presents early.

Now about this girl Jean. I understand your feelings.
There was a girl in my life too. Under no circumstances
must you withdraw from the play. There is an old
Greek saying: 'it is not by running away from evil that
we overcome it but by going to meet it.' Not that Jean
is evil in the sense implied or indeed in any sense but if
you fail to come to terms with this problem what chance
will you have against the harsher and weightier problems that will beset you as the years go by. No Joe.
Withdrawing from the play will not help you dismiss
Jean.

Anyhow you are doing no wrong. You think of the
girl a lot. You favour her beauty and seek her company.
She intrudes on your meditations and capriciously she
invades your studies. This is all natural and you must
not think that yours is an isolated or even an exceptional case.

Let us face squarely up to the problem. You say your
friendship with Jean is something special. I would expect it to be nothing else. She is a beautiful and
intelligent young girl. You are a handsome and brilliant
young man. You became attracted to each other inevitably but you must now ask yourself what is the
value of such an attraction. You must ask yourself if it
has a spiritual worth. To the latter I would answer yes
because it is a pure friendship. It will ennoble you at
least and properly cultivated the ultimate outcome must
be sublimity.

Let us take the phrase 'properly cultivated.' By this
is meant the effort to knock the last ha'porth as it were

out of a friendship and so develop it into something worthwhile. Your best efforts then should be directed towards adapting this fine friendship so that it will not harass your vocation but rather strengthen it.

If the girl causes you anguish or pain, if there is a spiritual ache then you must succumb or you must adopt a tough and resilient approach. You must find a pocket for this girl in the mental apparel of your vocation, a pocket which will contain her until time erases the charm she holds for you.

There is no shame in succumbing. She is a devout and pure girl and would make a splendid wife. Indeed purely from a selfish point of view I would favour this. I would like the company of children and love to have you and your wife near me in my declining years but I think Joe that you were cut out for the priesthood. I cannot see you truly happy in any other situation. I think we both know this.

Anyhow think on what I've said and we'll talk further at Christmas.

Your affectionate Uncle,
Martin O'Mora.

. . . .

Church Street,
Lochnanane.

Dear Father O'Mora,
Since I last wrote to you the position has not changed. The banging at the piano goes on till all hours every night. If you care to look into the dustbin at the back of Redlap's any Thursday, that's the collection day, you will see the empty brandy bottles.

I don't mind a person having a drink and a bit of a sing-song but this whacks all. It was half past two this very morning of the day I'm writing. It was fine outside and she came to the door with him when he was leaving. Talk about laughing and skitting. As he passed up I

54

said 'Good night, Father.' 'Ah 'tis you is it,' he said cheerily, 'you can go to bed now. I'm going home.'

Devotedly,
One who tries to be a good Catholic.

       .   .   .   .

The Dispensary,
Lochnanane.

Dear Father O'Mora,
I await your apology. I do not want to write to the bishop but if the apology is not forthcoming by return post that is exactly what I will do.

Sincerely,
Moffy, M.B.

       .   .   .   .

The Presbytery,
Lochnanane.

Dear Ray,
I've just left the courthouse where the dance-hall extensions were reviewed by Cormac O'Lunaigh, the circuit court judge. I'm afraid I fared badly. Grattan, the proprietor of the dance-hall, applied for twenty-four extensions till the hour of one o'clock in the morning. On the instructions of the bishop I opposed.

'Why do you oppose?' O'Lunaigh asked.
'Because the bishop instructed me to do so.'
'And why did he instruct you to do so?'
'Because the hours are too late.'
'What is your personal opinion?' he asked.

'I think that any boy or girl should have enough danced at twelve o'clock. It really is a question of morals.'

55

'What,' said he with a sneer, 'is the difference between the morals of the diocese of Limerick and your diocese, Father?'

'No difference,' I said.

'Then how is it?' he asked, 'that it is permissible to dance all the year round in Limerick till one o'clock in the morning but not in Lochnanane, or so your bishop and yourself would have it.'

'I'm afraid,' I said, 'I cannot answer that.'

'I see,' he said and he peered at me for my reactions. He also peered at Grattan for his. I must say that Grattan looked aggrieved and despondent. He wore a coat with frayed sleeves, a ragged shirt without a collar and a week's beard. There was a suggestion of a tear in one eye. He was a sorry sight. You would never think that a month before he offered forty thousand pounds for a farm.

'This poor man must not be deprived of his livelihood,' said O'Lunaigh. 'I hereby grant the extensions.'

It was Grattan's demeanour and dress that carried the day for him plus of course his reactions whenever the judge peered at him in that penetrating way that judges have who keep their heads down during most of a trial.

I don't care who the judge is or how learned he is or even if he was appointed on merit (that'll be the day) he will be deceived by reaction. A witness of Grattan's sort is masterly in cunning and has his reactions carefully rehearsed. The judge knew too that it would be a popular decision. He cutely cautioned Grattan that if he abused the privilege that Grattan would suffer for it. In this way O'Lunaigh was hugging the shores of authority and exhibiting the same sort of duplicity as the knaves who put him where he is. See you Friday.

As ever,
Martin.

• • • • • • • • • • •

Church Street,
Lochnanane.

Dear Father O'Mora,
I see that the hours get later by your curate. There is
no singing now. All is quiet and one gets suspicious
about what is going on. What can they be doing all
alone together for four and five hours at a time. Is it
right or natural? I thought in writing to you that it
would stop. At least when they were singing we knew
what they were at but what are they doing now?
    I think the bishop must be made to know of this
carry-on since you seem not to care one way or the
other.

Obediently,
One who tries to be a good Catholic.

*　　*　　*　　*　　*　　*　　*　　*　　*　　*　　*

The Presbytery,
Lochnanane.

Dear Doctor Moffy,
I will never apologise. It would be the same as
apologising for my religion. Anyhow I would not dream
of bending the knee to a cur.

Yours in J.C.,
Martin O'Mora, P.P.

*　　*　　*　　*　　*　　*　　*　　*　　*　　*　　*

The Presbytery,
Lochnanane.

Dear Joe,
All is back to normal here after Christmas. The curate
would put you off your breakfast with his eyes back in
his head from being up all night. When I attempt to
say something he raises a hand reproachfully and

motions me to silence. For the sake of harmony I say nothing till lunchtime. Yesterday I told him he was keeping very erratic hours, hours that might be injurious to his health. 'We must not think of ourselves,' he answered mockingly and sanctimoniously, 'I always put parish duties before my health. That is what the priesthood is all about.'

So saying he rose unsteadily and in a series of moves something like those of an attacking Fijian rugby fullback negotiated the door. I saw no more of him till supper time when he appeared fresh, sober and in excellent fettle. He went off to hear confessions. I'm sure that's where he gets the money. He is a great hand with the ladies but to me are left the hundred and one duties that make up the successful running of a parish. Today it might be the giving of a pledge to a drunkard who beats his wife. Tomorrow could find me knocking at the door of a house to break the news of a traffic accident. The father of a young family may have been killed while cycling home from work or a mother and child killed when their car was struck by a lorry. The day after I might be consoling the mother of a son who has just been jailed for theft or violence. This very moment the phone might ring with news of a disaster for some unfortunate family. I often ask myself why does God let these things happen and I am stymied for an answer. Accepting God's will is never easy for those who suffer. God is the only scapegoat who does not defend himself.

You asked in your letter for the story of the Castlekellingham Come-Uppance. It's a long story; perhaps during the next few months.

Speaking about confessions reminds me of our late friend Canon Dring of Killaveg. Canon Dring would never hear confessions for the good reason that he did not benefit financially in the box. The result was that the curate Tom Kilmartin was always stuck and could never go home to nourish himself over a long week-end. Eventually he thought of a number. After leaving the confessional one night he went into the presbytery kitchen where the housekeeper Nellie Dwan was sitting by a pale fire. In Nellie's presence he started to take bundles of pound notes (borrowed) from his pockets. Then half to himself he said 'I'll never get all these masses said.'

Needless to say Nellie reported at once to Canon Dring. Father Tom was relieved of confessional duties there and then and Canon Dring took over.

I must raise seven thousand pounds shortly. The National School needs to be extended. There is no doubt but that the Department of Education has right hares made out of the Parish Priests of Ireland. I am a school manager. In addition I am expected to build schools. I inspect schools regularly yet I receive no salary from the Department although I am worth them at least three thousand pounds a year. I don't know why I do it unless it is in the best interests of the children.

We are expected to appoint teachers, to interview them and often provide houses for them, yet not a penny in return. All I ever made by appointing teachers was a dangerous huddle of enemies in the persons of those I didn't appoint. A teacher in the sulks is a deceptive and unpredictable adversary as you will find out all too soon. I would sooner wrestle an orang-outang than face a deluded schoolmaster. There was once a teacher from Castlepellick with the mad eyes of a sparrow-hawk who threatened to shoot his parish priest. Apparently the priest appointed somebody else to be school principal. The priest died suddenly. Some said he died with the fright but the mother of the losing candidate said he was struck down by the hand of God.

Two daffodils have just shown their orange ears at the lee of the house. I expect that they shall be followed shortly by hundreds of others. Write soon.

Your affectionate uncle,
Martin O'Mora, P.P.

*   *   *   *   *   .   .   .   *   .   .

59

Bishop's House.

Memo. to Father Martin O'Mora.

Martin,
Two disturbing letters to hand. One has to do with your
curate. Speak to him or I will. Have it out to the end
with him and no pussy-footing. The other is from
Doctor Moffy. I cannot make you do anything against
your will but I suggest you do the big thing and
apologise.

You are doing great work. When the extension is
built I may have something in mind for you. Keep up
the good work.

In haste,
Mick.

*   *   *   *   *   *   *   *   *   *   *

The Presbytery,
Lochnanane.

Dear Doctor Moffy,
I apologise unreservedly for my recent behaviour
towards you. I sincerely hope you will see your way to
forgiving me.

Sincerely,
Martin O'Mora, P.P.

*   *   *   *   *   *   *   *   *

The Dispensary,
Lochnanane.

Dear Father O'Mora,
All is forgiven.

Moffy, M.B.

*   *   *   *   *   *   *   *   *

Dear Ray,

I am after a session with my curate which beats all I
ever experienced. The session was not initiated by yours
truly. There was a sharp memo from the boss, a sort
of do-it-or-else injunction which could not be ignored.
I decided to wait for him this very morning. At two-
fifteen I heard his key in the lock. In the hallway he
shook the hailstones from his hat and from the
shoulders of his overcoat. He could and should have
disposed of these hailstones before coming indoors but
he is of a very perverse and vexatious nature. He
headed in the general direction of the kitchen singing
'Beneath thy Window.' After a few minutes I followed
him to the kitchen where he was eating tinned salmon
and a few slices of bread and butter. He produced a
bottle of beer from his trousers pocket, opened it and
poured it into a glass. It was then he saw me for the
first time.

'Come in, come in,' he called expansively. I was
already in at this stage.

'Have a seat,' he invited. Then he motioned to the
victuals. 'Help yourself,' he said. I took a seat and said
nothing for a while. I could see that he was nicely
although he was far from being drunk.

'This is a great little country we're living in,' he
announced. I decided to wait a while longer before
acquainting him of my purpose.

'Where would you get butter the like of this,' he said
and he held a lump aloft on his knife. 'Or tell me,' he
went on, 'where would you find a curate drinking beer
and eating tinned salmon at this hour. I tell you we
don't half appreciate this country. You are very serious
looking, Father. Is there to be some sort of con-
frontation?'

'Finish your snack,' I advised him.

'Oh I would be doing that anyway,' he said with a
shake of the head. 'I never let anything interfere with
my eating. No future in it. There are too many honest

61

men suffering from ulcers.' He was enjoying himself immensely at my expense. Finally he finished off the salmon, the bread and the beer. He then wiped his mouth with a dishcloth.

'Well, now,' he said, 'let's hear from you.' With that he folded his arms and closed his eyes. 'I can concentrate better with my eyes shut,' he explained.

'There have been letters,' I said.

'I know,' he said, 'and what is more I know from whom.'

'You know more than I do,' I told him. 'Anyhow,' I went on, 'there have been letters from other sources.' He laughed at this. 'I didn't realise I was so famous,' he said.

'The bishop,' I said, cutting in on him, 'has asked me to talk to you.'

'About what?' he asked.

'About your comings and goings at all hours of the morning,' I said, 'about keeping company with a woman when the whole village is in bed. About staggering on the village street blind drunk on occasion.'

'What woman?' he asked.

'Miss Daisy Redlap,' I told him. He rubbed his jaw at this, opened his eyes and pursed his lips. It was obvious that he had more drink taken than I first thought.

'Miss Daisy Redlap,' he repeated.

'Yes,' I said.

'Does this mean I am not to see her again?'

'It would look like it,' I told him.

'Who is going to prevent me from seeing her?' he asked.

'The bishop,' I said.

'It's a free country,' he said, 'and if the bishop don't like the way I come and go that's tough cheese on the bishop.'

I must confess, Ray, that I was shocked at this. 'Do you realise what you are saying?' I entreated him.

'No better man,' he said and he rose from the table. 'You can tell the bishop from me,' he shouted, 'that if he don't mind his own business I might jack the whole thing up.'

'You are drunk,' I said, 'you don't realise what you are saying. We'll talk in the morning when you are sober.'

He pushed me back on to the chair.

'We will talk now,' he roared at the top of his voice. 'If I hear as much as another word out of you or the bloody bishop I'll blow the hell out of here to England and get a job teaching. I might even take Daisy with me.'

'You're mad,' I told him, 'you realise I will have to report all this to the bishop.'

'Man dear,' he laughed, 'I don't give a tinker's curse about the bishop. This is a free country. There is nothing you or the bishop can do to me. I wish I had another bottle of beer.'

I tried a change of tune.

'Daisy Redlap,' I advised him, 'is twice your age.'

'Lies,' he roared. 'Lies.'

'She is over fifty,' I told him. 'You are only twenty-seven.'

'You're jealous,' he said. He then grabbed me by the throat.

'If you so much as mention her name again,' he threatened, 'I'll guzzle you. He was obviously out of his mind on the occasion so I said nothing. He released me suddenly.

'Sorry,' he said, 'I shouldn't have done that.'

Without another word he went upstairs to bed. Over the breakfast table I told him that I would forget about the night before if he promised to keep fairly regular hours and cut down on his drinking.

'I'll do what I can,' he promised. He seemed to mean it but then his attitude changed.

'Dammit,' he said, 'I want to be honest with you. It was my mother the bitch who made me into a priest. I hadn't the guts or the manliness to stand up to her. She used to boast about me. Lies every word. I lived a lie all the time. I'm living a lie now.'

'We've all had our problems,' I tried to console

him. 'Yours could turn you into a great priest. Problems solve themselves as the months go by.'

'I still have mine,' he cried almost in tears. 'Do you think that I don't know that Daisy Redlap is older than I. I still want her and I can't drive her from my thoughts. I've always wanted women. I loved their softness, their bulging whiteness. I've craved for them, I've screamed in my anguish for them. That's what I see in Daisy Redlap. She's bulging and plump and white beyond words, beyond my wildest dreams. Sometimes when she barely stirs she shudders and shivers all over. Her trembling tortures me when she moves from one place to another.'

'You will have to go on retreat,' I told him, 'there is no other way.'

He calmed down at once.

'I suppose you're right,' he said.

'I'll arrange it,' I told him.

'Yes, yes,' he whispered, 'do that for me Father.'

He arose and withdrew. I presume he will re-appear at supper. I heard through the grapevine that you are having chest pains again. Take care and rest. I will take you to see a friend of mine in Cork next week-end. Good men are scarce. Be ready early on Sunday afternoon. I'll ring tomorrow or after.

As usual,
Martin.

•   ¶   •   ⁋   ⁂   •   ⁎   ⁜   •   •

St. Unshin's,
Ballyrango.

Dear Uncle Martin,

The play opened last night and went well. We started shakily which is understandable since we had time only for one dress rehearsal. As the night wore on, however, we really got to grips with it and afterwards everybody agreed that we had done an excellent job considering our limitations. A few of the lads here have varying accounts of the Castlekellingham Come-Uppance. I promised I would ask you for the correct version. When did it happen? Who was involved? Is it considered a scandal etc.? I realise how busy you must be with your curate the way he is but if you got a chance some night I would really appreciate if you sat down and wrote us an account of it. Give my fond regards to herself.

> As ever,
> Your affectionate nephew,
> Joe.

. . . .

> The High Valleys,
> Lochnanane.

Dear Father O'Mora,
I am a married woman whose family is done for and all gone their ways abroad in the world from their home in the High Valleys. My husband and I were always united and happy until two months ago he got a parcel from his brother Martin in Chicago. First I thought the contents was a rubber boat or the like but I found out in time it was a rubber woman that could be pumped up with air or filled with warm water until it became the size and shape and colour of a fine figure of a young woman exactly the same in appearance as Dolores Viago, the famous film star that was in voyage to mars. She has glass eyes, dark with long lashes exactly the same as the real Dolores and when she is squeezed she sighs like a real person from some gadget under her oxter. My husband has gone crazy over her, taking her to bed and talking to her and buying the like of a watch for her and some nice clothes and underwear. I do not know what to do Father. There are more cases than me here in the High Valleys which was always a holy and contented place where the Rosary is never

missed in any house even still but he puts Dolores
Viago in the trimmings and puts her alongside him
and says a decade in a woman's voice, by the way it
would be her talking. He answers in his own voice
and I answer too for the sake of quietness. Others have
their false women too but it was my brother-in-law
Martin that sent the first one. Then they all started writing for one. I only saw one other. She is the image of
Mrs. Freddie Fox-Pelley who rides the horses on T.V.
except she hasn't a stitch of clothes on her.

Will you guide us Father out of this evil pass. Pray
for us Father. Our men are shoving into the years and
are turning a bit foolish. Frighten them Father know
would they forget this nonsense.

Yours faithfully,
Noreen Hannassy (Mrs.).

*   ·   ·   ·   ·   ·   ·   ·   ·   ·

The Presbytery,
Lochnanane.

Dear Joe,

Always great to hear from you. The greatest poker
player that ever lived, in the opinion of those who
ought to know, was the late Father Fonsie Lynd of
Lackira. A few others preferred the late Dynamite
Carey who was an authority on the finer points of the
game. Dynamite was often consulted where there were
no rules of the house. Fonsie was a tight-fisted man
but you could not call him mean. He had great points.
His is another instance of a missing fortune. When he
died there was no trace of his money save for a few
hundred pounds in his bank account. I'll tell you something which I was once told by the administrator of a
certain diocese in Germany.

She assured me that a certain Swiss Bank was bulging with the money of more than a few Irish P.P.s

who over-estimated their lives' spans. In answer to your major question let me assure you that the 'Come-Uppance' was not a scandal. Every diocese has its scandal but this is not ours.

Anyhow Fonsie Lynd was one of the Principals of the Castlekellingham Come-Uppance. Jim Lollery, the County Engineer was another. My dear friend Father Ray Tubridy was a third. Ray is not well by the way. His chest pains continue, growing worse all the time. The fourth was a close friend of mine, a shopkeeper named Neddy Lackin. The fifth was Doctor Petey Wyse and the final member of the once famous Castlekellingham poker school was your beloved uncle whose hand is to this letter.

During the long winter months we would meet, the six of us, in the Castlekellingham C.Y.M.S. Hall where we would play a modest game on Monday and Thursday nights. We did not play in the common room of the hall but in the caretaker's office, a cosy place with a bright turf fire. It was at the rear of the building. The game was usually of the two-shillings-up-the-dealer variety but some of us would skip deals if the action was dull. Often we would have a last pot for a pound-up-the-dealer. A loser might recoup all his night's losses if he won this, the last and most valuable pot. The night of the Come-Uppance as it is now called was the fourth night of January nine years ago. We had not met since before Christmas and we were anxious for a game.

I won the first pot. I won it with a flush of clubs against Doctor Petey Wyse who had two pair and Neddy Lackin who had small trips. It was the hottest game of poker I ever played from the third hand on. Every player was involved all the way through but steadily, surely the money started to drift towards the maestro, Father Fonsie Lynd. The heaviest loser was Jim Lollery, which was a pity, because he was a poor loser, being notoriously short-tempered and tight-fisted. It is also a part of diocesan poker history that he hated Fonsie Lynd's guts. He had lost too much to him over the years.

It wanted five minutes to twelve so we decided to play the last pot. It was Fonsie's deal. He paused for a moment and then he threw a five pound note on the table. 'The dealer makes it a fiver,' he announced 'and I am skipping.'

He handed the cards to Lollery who threw up a fiver and also skipped his deal. Out of sheer bravado we all skipped so that there were thirty pounds in the pot. It was Ray's deal. Kings were openers and as he dealt his hands trembled. Slowly he counted out the cards. Every face was pale except that of Father Fonsie Lynd. Fonsie was the same as always. He belonged at where he was at. He was master of the situation. After an agonising two minutes the cards were dealt out. Every man clutched his allowance of five and slowly each prized his apart.

'It's open,' said Father Fonsie with a ring of triumph in his voice. He produced his wallet and extracted fifteen pounds. 'Anyone who wants to play,' he said, 'plays for fifteen pounds.'

Slowly, almost painfully wads and wallets were produced. All of us signified our intention of playing with him. We placed our stakes in the pot. All looked in the direction of Jim Lollery who had made no decision or had given no indication of any kind that he was playing. He looked at the pot and moistened his lips. He repeated this gesture over and over until he had fully surveyed the terrain.

'Alright,' he said in a tone which it was difficult to associate with him in normal circumstances. 'I am hardening this pot to thirty quid.'

Some sighed but all showed their willingness to participate. Duly the pot was filled until in the centre of the table was a heap of notes totalling two hundred and ten pounds.

Discards were thrown to one side and the filling of hands commenced.

Father Fonsie Lynd bought three cards to a pair of kings. I bought one card to a nine high straight. Neddy bought one card to four of a flush. Doc Wyse bought three to a pair of knaves. Jim Lollery bought two to three deuces and Ray who was dealer and last for cards bought one card to sevens and eights. Carefully he put the remainder of the cards aside. It was up to Fonsie Lynd. It was he who opened the pot. Fonsie was never a man for beating about the bush.

'I'll bet a hundred,' he said. So saying he produced his cheque book, took one out, signed it and threw the blank cheque on top of the pot. This was teetotally unprecedented. It was frightening.

All threw in their cards except one man. That man's name was Jim Lollery. He placed his to one side and rubbed his hands together. A smile showed on his face.

'Did you say a hundred?' he asked.

'I believe I did,' said Fonsie without batting an eyelid.

'I'll tell you what I'll do,' said Lollery, 'I'll make it two.'

'Four,' said Fonsie as if he were passing the time of day. I felt like pinching myself. A four hundred pound pot on a two-shilling-up-the-dealer game of poker? Was I dreaming. 'Boys,' said Ray in a shaking voice, 'let this be the end of it. The fun is gone from our game. Withdraw the bets and let the better of the two of you take the pot. Divide it if necessary.'

'Keep out of this you fool,' Lollery directed at him.

'Sorry Ray,' said Fonsie cutting in sharply on Lollery. 'But a bet is a bet. I am making it four hundred pounds Lollery. Are you looking or aren't you?'

'I am making it eight hundred pounds, Father,' Lollery said coldly and with this he located his cheque book. He signed the cheque and wrote out the amount. He placed the cheque directly in front of Fonsie.

Fonsie never batted an eyelid. 'That's a lot of money,' he mused without showing the slightest sign of emotion.

'Fill the amount in your cheque if you want to look at my hand,' Lollery told him. 'It's getting late and I can wait no longer.' He pretended he was about to sweep in the pot. Fonsie withdrew his cheque from the middle of the heap and filled it in.

'Declare,' Fonsie ordered.

'Two pairs,' said Lollery with a grin.

'Too bad,' said Fonsie. 'I have a full house consisting of kings on the roof.' He put down his cards and was about to draw in the pot when Lollery intercepted him.

'You mustn't have heard me right,' he said.

'I heard you loud and clear,' said Fonsie, 'you said you had two pairs. I have a full house and a full house beats two pairs anytime.'

'I accept that,' said Lollery with a broad grin, 'but my two pairs are two pairs of deuces.' So saying he threw down the four deuces where everybody could see them. Then he proceeded to haul in the pot which at this stage totalled one thousand eight hundred and ten pounds.

'Hold it right there mister,' Fonsie announced suddenly. 'You declared two pairs. I declared a house. I don't care if you have four deuces. I am judging your hand by what you declared. You declared you had two pairs of deuces. You therefore lose the pot. Someone muttered approval although the rest of us felt that Fonsie's assertion was outrageous and ridiculous. 'Absolute rubbish,' Lollery laughed and he made a second attempt to gather his winnings. It was then that Fonsie stood up. He spoke slowly.

'That pot is mine,' he said, 'and anybody who thinks otherwise is asking for trouble.'

Lollery looked for redress from one of our faces to another and although most of us felt that the pot should be his we showed no sympathy. There was a stalemate. Lollery was nonplussed.

'Look,' he said, 'will you stop doing the fool and let me rake in my lawful winnings.'

'They are not lawful,' Fonsie insisted. So the argument wore on for over an hour. At length it was agreed by both parties that the issue should be decided by Father Donal (Dynamite) Carey. Lollery was confident that he would get the verdict. So was I. So were the others excepting Neddy. It was exactly three weeks to the day before Dynamite dropped dead. We found him in his study at 1.30 a.m. reading Honore de Balzac. There was a bottle of whiskey by his side and a half filled glass in one of his hands. He was surprised to see us but he received us warmly.

'Martin,' he said to me, 'pour the boys a shot of the Goddam dynamite.'

I filled drinks all round and on his instructions replenished his own glass. We sat down. From my pocket I withdrew the stake money. I placed it on a table and laid bare the facts of the case as best I could. Dynamite listened carefully and when I had concluded he put me one question.

'Does the C.Y.M.S. Hall have house rules, Martin?' I told him no.

'Are both parties fully agreed to accept my verdict?' he asked. Both assured him that they were.

'Boys,' said he, 'I played poker in half the states of the Union. I saw a man shot dead for falsely declaring a flush of hearts. The flush had one diamond. Still that is not a precedent for judgment in this case. Be that as it may there are thousands of precedents. In the absence of house rules the declared hand is the lawful hand. Mr. Lollery you found yourself with four deuces yet you declared that you had two pairs. The reason you did this was that you wanted Father Lynd to believe, however temporarily, that two pairs was all you had. Not satisfied with winning you also wanted to play a game of cat and mouse with your victim. This is precisely why there is a little-known but internationally accepted rule in poker known as the come-uppance. Where it began I cannot say but it is a fact that gentlemen everywhere abide by it. I have played poker since boyhood but at no time in my life did I ask a man for a look at his cards. I always accepted what he declared. A gentleman's word is his be-all and end-all so that if you declared two pairs of deuces to me Mr. Lollery it would be final and I would take it for granted that you had two pairs. Acceptance of declaration is a hard and fast rule where men of honour foregather to play poker. Those who break the rule must pay the price. I therefore award the pot to Father Lynd.'

Lollery protested but it was pointed out to him that he had agreed to accept the findings, whatever they might be. He left without a word. As far as I know he never played poker thereafter. I hope this true story of the Castlekellingham Come-Uppance pleases your pals.

Your affectionate Uncle,
Martin O'Mora, P.P.

*   *   *   *   *   *   *   *   *   *

The Presbytery,
Lochnanane.

Dear Ray,

The following is the short history of what I will lightly call the High Valleys Heresy. A few weeks ago I received a distraught letter from a Mrs. Noreen Hannassy about which I told you. It concerned a rubber woman as you will remember. First I was going to enlist the aid of a few Redemptorists and let them loose in the High Valleys but those days are gone and more's the pity. I arrived at Hannassy's not long after receiving the letter. They were just finishing the midday meal.

At the table was Mrs. Hannassy, Mr. Jack Hannassy and his friend Dolores Viago, the rubber woman. I must confess she looked very lifelike and in all respects that I could notice resembled the famous film star of the same name. Dolores sat upright with both hands in front of her on the table. She wore a purple trouser suit, bought for her by Jack. Jack and the wife stood up as soon as I entered but he made no attempt to hide Dolores. Mrs. Hannassy invited me to take a seat and at once she started to cry. She attempted to dry her tears with her apron but lost control of her weeping, stood up and turned towards the door.

'You're not like that,' said Jack to Dolores, 'always crying and stinking.' So saying he gave Dolores a kiss on the cheek.

'Destroy that evil image,' I roared at him, 'or I'll have you excommunicated.'

To this he made no answer. Instead he lifted Dolores Viago in his arms and took her to the bedroom. There he proceeded to strip her. I intervened and further warned him about excommunication but he roughly pushed me to one side. Stripped of her garments this rubber object turned out to be as fine a physical female as you could behold. In every manner imaginable she resembled a naked woman. He drew back the bedclothes and laid her down gently. He then drew the clothes over her body. Then he proceeded to undress himself. He ignored my presence. I pleaded with him to have respect for his wife and religion but his eyes were glazed with lustful longing. I left him to his devilish work and went from the room to console his unfortunate spouse.

She informed me that many of the men of the High Valleys had rubber women which resembled famous female personalities and film stars. Here was a pretty kettle of fish. I could think of nothing in the civil law to stop them unless alone a charge of cruelty could be brought against them. But then we would be the talk of the civilised world as they call it and that would never do.

Mrs. Hannassy gave me the names of the other miscreants and I spent a fruitless evening trying to make them see the light. If word of what was going on ever got outside the High Valleys we would never live it down in the parish of Lochnanane. Towards the end of my journey I came to the house of an octogenarian whose name was Alaphonsus Maclir. It was he who owned the image of Mrs. Freddie Fox-Pelley, the famous horsewoman. Up to the time I arrived he had not been able to blow her up to lifesize or fill her with warm water. He hadn't sufficient vessels for the latter or the car pump required for the former. When I arrived he was pumping away with a pump which had been loaned him by a neighbour. The job was near completion as I entered. Remember that the scoundrel was eighty-three years of age. His old woman, Tessie, sat doting in the corner while the neighbour, a man in his fifties, looked on. They ignored my presence despite my pointing out to them the evil they were manufacturing.

When Mrs. Freddie Fox-Pelley was blown up I must say she was a breath-taking sight. The neighbour flung his hands about her abdomen but Alaphonsus Maclir with a vicious blow to the mouth drove him back. 'Bide your time, bide your time,' he shouted, 'you'll get your turn.' The old man looked every bit as hideous as a West African, rib nosed baboon when he bore her to the bedroom. I left in disgust wondering how I would combat this dreadful plague. I was hardly fifty yards from the house when the neighbour called after me franticaly. 'Come quick. Come quick Father,' he shouted at the top of his voice. I returned to the house. There in the arms of Mrs. Freddie Fox-Pelley lay the corpse of Alaphonsus Maclir. The effort had been too much for him or maybe it was God in his wrath.

When word of his sudden demise spread every rubber woman in the High Valleys was burned or cut into pieces. I think they have learned their lesson. Can you, by the wildest and most vivid use of your excellent imagination, hazard a guess at how the Protestant-owned English Sunday newspapers would treat a story like this? I shudder to think of it. I cross myself hourly and thank God for our narrow escape.

I hope you are obeying the specialist's orders. Plenty of rest and no excitement. I will be out to see you some time Sunday night.

As ever,
Martin.

. . . .

St. Unshin's College,
Ballyrango.

Dear Uncle Martin,
All goes well and I have now dismissed Jean from my
mind although there are vestiges of pain and thoughts
that nearly wrench out my heart. We still meet and
have chats from time to time in the debating hall.
Your advice was invaluable. Summer draws near
and there will be five of the lads for ordination. My
turn next year D.V. I think I will go to England and
get a job this summer if it is alright with you. A pal
of mine will come with me. It will be good experience
apart from the money we will earn. One of the pro-
fessors here told me part of a yarn about the funeral
rehearsal of a Father Bosco McNelly. You must tell
me all about it when I get home. There is no news
from this place, so for the present I will close. I look
forward very much to hearing from you.

Your affectionate nephew,
Joe.

*   *   .   .   .   .

Church Street,
Lochnanane.

Dear Father O'Mora,
The lull is over. They are at it again till two and three
in the morning. Long, long mysterious silences that
baffle a person. This curate is walking on the razor
blade's edge. I hope you told him Daisy Redlap's
age while you were at it. I knew their parting couldn't
last. I would swear in a court of law that she made
him take Coaxiorum. He has the look of it in his
eyes. I wouldn't put it past her. I heard there was no
cure for Coaxiorum except some sort of psalm read
in Latin by the bishop. I never see two that wanted
the Latin so badly. It was half two this very morning

75

when I heard the door banging. I went downstairs for a breath of air.

'Nice night, Father,' I said as he passed by.

'Ah yes, my child,' he said sarcastic like, 'it surely is for half two in the morning.'

'I didn't see you this long while, Father,' said I to him.

'I know,' he said. 'I know and you can be assured that it will be a thousand times as long before you will see me again, you or anyone else in this prying place.'

I'm just tipping you off, Father. When he's under the spell of Coaxiorum there's no telling what he'll do.

> One who tries to be a good
> Catholic.

•　 ,　 ｇ　 ｕ　 ,　 ｓ　 ｙ　 ｘ　 ｃ　 ｖ　 •

> The Presbytery,
> Lochnanane.

Dear Joe,

As a rule mine is a lonely life although a happy one in the spiritual sense; being the busiest man in the parish does not make it less lonely. It is now but four o'clock in the afternoon and here is a list of what had to be attended to this day so far.

First a visit from one of the greatest thieves in the diocese, a gentleman with twenty convictions for larceny, requesting a reference for a job as cashier in a Limerick supermarket. I sent him about his business quickly. Next came the post with a letter from a parishioner who wants her name and the names of her children and husband changed to her maiden name. I suggested she visit a solicitor. A second letter from a woman who signs herself 'One who tries to be a good Catholic'. I hope she doesn't try any harder.

Then there was a visit from a mother whose son would not get up for mass on Sunday mornings. I advised her to starve him for a while. It always works.

Next a visit from the secretary of the local cumann of the Fianna Fáil Party for permission to hold a church gate collection. I agreed. That was a great song, that 'Forty Shades of Green'. I wonder if the political parties are included, each one trying to be greener than the next. Then a visit from a young married woman who told me that her husband would not make love to her. She brought him along and he declared that he had been promised two heifers by the girl's father the day after the marriage. The months passed but the heifers never materialised. I advised him to go home and to make love to his wife and forget about the heifers.

'No Father,' he said, 'blast the button will I open till I get my two heifers.' He left satisfied when I told him I would talk to his father-in-law. I presume the wife has no complaints now.

Next a visit from a girl home from England wanting me to marry her to a Protestant who was not prepared to change his religion, which he never practised anyway. I showed her the door and told her I would pray for her. Marriage is tough enough without mixing it. Next a visit from a mother who told me that her daughter was doing a line with a married man. I promised to talk to the girl. Next came a farmer who claimed that some person with the evil eye was working pishogues against his stock. His calves and fowl were dying mysteriously. He isn't the first bad farmer to blame pishogues. I promised to visit his place, and now on top of all I must go to the convent and hear the nuns' confessions. You mention the famous funeral rehearsal of Father Bosco McNally. Joe, it was no yarn. I'll tell you all about it in my next letter. Meanwhile the very best to you in everything. You will find a tenner enclosed.

> Your affectionate Uncle,
> Martin O'Mora, P.P.

Dear Father O'Mora,

More than me now knows about the carry-on. Man,
woman and child in the street knows that he is courting Daisy Redlap. She is a hard creature to be egging
him on and wearing minis that would suit someone the
third of her age. She came to the door the other night
in a bikini when I knocked to find out the time. My
own clock is stopped.

'What are you wearing the bikini for?' I asked.

'Himself is helping me pick out one,' she said, 'I got
eight pairs altogether on appro. I think I'll keep this
one,' she laughed and she hit herself a slap on the belly.
'He likes it the best.' The next thing she did was to
bang the door in my face.

What do you think of that, Father? Is there a
sacrilege being committed in a Catholic Street?

One who tries to be a
good Catholic.

   ạ   ᴣ   •   ᴣ   ᴣ   ᴣ   ʸ   :   •   •   •

The Presbytery,
Lochnanane.

Dear Ray,

The inevitable has happened. My curate, Father Carrity, has succumbed to the prodigious guiles and
quaking white form of Daisy Redlap. Caveat emptor.
He started the shenanigans less than a week after he
came home from his Retreat. In the face of a growing
storm by pious lay folk who were witnessing his
gradual and carnal downfall I called him aside and
spoke to him as follows.

'Father,' I said, 'why persecutest thou me? Have I
not given you a fair break? Have I not been the

epitome of paternity and the very soul of indulgence? I placed my trust in you Father and you failed me. I appealed to your nobler nature and you betrayed me.'

He yawned and pandiculated himself on the chair. 'I'm tired,' he said. 'For that reason I will not elaborate on the tidings I have for you.'

'What tidings?' I demanded. 'What nonsense is this? You show scant courtesy to your Parish Priest.'

'I'm jacking the whole thing up and going off with Daisy,' he said. 'As of now I am one of those pious layfolk you so often refer to.' With that he whipped the collar from his neck and threw it on the table.

'Dogs who wear collars have my sympathy,' he crowed. He stood up and fondled his double chin.

'The noose is gone from around my neck,' he declared.

'It could be that you are swapping one noose for another,' I warned him. 'Anyhow you just can't walk out of your ministry in a flash. There is more to leaving than that, a lot more.'

'There may be,' he said, 'but not for me. I have no qualms of conscience whatsoever. I have lived in an arid and musty world for most of my life, from seminary to college to parish. I am no longer the lapdog of Latin lunacy. I'm a free man.'

'Your mother,' I reminded him. 'This will be the death of the poor woman.'

'Amen,' said he.

'Stand right where you are,' I commanded him, 'and I will ring the bishop this very minute.'

'The bishop is in Lourdes,' he said, 'and damn well you know it. Now I must be off. My bags are packed and Daisy awaits me.'

'If you refuse to think of yourself,' I pleaded, 'think of the unfortunate wretch you are dragging into the mire with you."

'What mire?' he shouted, 'you talk like a mad missioner out of the starving thirties. You offend me when you call my wife-to-be a wretch.'

'You are both mesmerised by lust,' I answered him. He laughed loudly upon hearing this.

'We have given it a lot of thought,' he said. 'We are agreed that many people are born into this world for the express purpose of suffering so we have decreed that we shall not be of these. Daisy's house is up for auction next week. My worldly goods are in my two suitcases which I deposited in the boot of my car yesterday. I'm sure you have work to do, Father,' he concluded, pulling a heinously coloured scarf from his trousers pocket and knotting it loosely around his neck. He then placed the key of the door on the table, shook my hand and skipped whistling to his car. That is the last I saw of him. I will say no more about him. I have yet to get over the shock of his departure. Church Street is still astounded.

The new curate is twenty-four years of age. He was ordained last year. His name is Michael Greary. I like him. He loves work, takes a pint or two with the local lads and is a very cheerful sort withal. What is more important is that Mary Teresa likes him and she has yet to be wrong. Father Carrity was only here a week when I asked her what she thought of him.

'He has the gamese of a latchico,' she said, 'the archrump of a finished idler and the soft neck of a Polly bull.' She has always been a great judge of character. She asks for you regularly. See you Sunday night.

As ever,
Martin.

•   ·   ■   ■   ■   ■   ■   ■   ▪   ▪   ◄

Church Street,
Lochnanane.

Dear Father O'Mora,

I am not going to start and say I told you so. The harm of the year go with the pair of them. Wait till he gets a right look at Daisy without her make-up some morning. The reason I take up my pen is to inform you that your new curate is to be seen drinking pints regularly at the Five Poplars with the local lads. What are priests coming to at all these days? The Five Poplars is a low and common pub often open for business till all hours of the morning. Another evening I saw him wear a green jumper on his way to the ball-alley with Tricky Micky Cade who is a wife stealer. It's well known that he sleeps at Rita Sinnon's all the year round except when her husband is home from England for a few weeks in the summer. I wonder will this curate turn out like the last. God knows he has made a good start.

One who tries to be a
good Catholic.

* * * * * * * * * * *

The Presbytery,
Lochnanane.

Dear Joe,

I promised I would write and tell you about the funeral rehearsal of Father Bosco McNelly, parish priest of Tooreenturk. Before I do let me tell you something about the beginnings. There might have been no funeral rehearsal if Bosco had not delivered an extremely crude sermon on the occasion of the bishop's visit to Tooreenturk for the confirmations of 1943. The funeral rehearsal is often confused with the German invasion of Tooreenturk which many local people say took place on the same day. Army authorities and the Department of Foreign Affairs strenuously deny that there was an invasion.

Anyhow the Catholic church of Tooreenturk was crowded to the doors when the bishop arrived. In the presbytery the bishop, together with several canons and Bosco donned vestments. The distinguished party then made its way to the church. It was a fine occasion and the procession was a happy one with much banter flowing back and forth. At the entrance to the nave the party halted for a moment and looked with disgust at a freshly discharged portion of human faeces. No word was said but Bosco was livid. When the bishop had delivered himself of his sermon Bosco went into the pulpit.

He began with Mesopotamia and told the congregation of the respect the people of that faraway, forgotten land had for their places of worship. He praised the Greeks and the Phoenicians for the same qualities. He also pointed out that none of these people were Christian. It was then he decided to address himself to the folk of Tooreenturk proper but in particular to the scoundrel who had relieved himself at the entrance to the church. He dwelt on the man's antecedents at great length, likening them to apes and gorillas. He cursed the seed and breed of the monster who had desecrated his church and accused him of sacrilege. He ordered him to stand up but needless to say nobody was foolish enough to do so. By this time the bishop was thoroughly annoyed by the long and unpleasant harangue. A half hour passed and people started to squirm but still Bosco extended his diatribe. Finally he approached the end. He pointed a finger towards the doorway.

'Let me say,' said he, 'that I take no exception to a man relieving himself if he is caught short. I have no objection to a sick person who cannot restrain himself but,' and here he was vehement, 'I had a good look at the heap outside the door of this church and I can safely say that it was the result, not of a sickly misfortune but of a mighty strenuous effort.'

The Bishop who was a sensitive man made a mental note never to attend at any ceremony in the parish of Tooreenturk until such time as Bosco had departed from it.

He conveyed his sentiments to his administrator and in due course word reached Bosco that he had truly incurred the wrath of the bishop.

In many respects Bosco was a simple man and the one thing he looked forward to most was his own funeral. Already he had selected a grave at a special corner of Tooreenturk Graveyard and already it was dug to a depth of six inches. He had also erected a huge Celtic Cross which bore his name, his year of birth and a quotation from Francis Thompson: 'Look For Me In The Nurseries Of Heaven.' Now all his hopes were dashed because he was certain that the bishop would never attend his funeral. He conveyed his worries to his parishioners who had a great regard for him whatever the bishop might think. They were agreed that without the bishop it would not be much of a funeral. Encouraged by his friends Bosco decided that he would take no chances. 'Look,' he said to a special committee which he had appointed to examine the matter, 'since I will not be here myself to supervise it we had better have a dress rehearsal.'

The committee was agreed. Word spread and the parish entered into the spirit of the thing. Tooreenturk was a quiet backwater and this was a great opportunity for the people to show that they were more than mere oafs. The rest is a fairly long story so I will postpone it for a few weeks when I will give you the final chapters, as it were, of the German Invasion of Tooreenturk.

Do you want for anything? Be sure to let me know. I think that going to England is a good idea. It is a Pagan country but there is much to be learned if you keep your eyes opened and refuse to be drawn.

As ever,
Your affectionate Uncle,
Martin O'Mora, P.P.

*   *   *   *   *   *   *   *   *   *

The Presbytery,
Lochnanane.

Dear Ray,
I hate to have to tell you that I noticed a decline in you on Sunday night. You will have to take things easy. Good men are scarce. My new curate is a great lad entirely. He has great patience with elderly people

and invalids and this is most important as we both
know. He is a man who can carry his drink. When I
arrived home on Sunday night after leaving you we
polished off the best part of a bottle of whiskey while
we reviewed the work of the Parish and re-established
our priorities. I showed him the letter I received from
our friend who is still trying to be a good Catholic
and he informed me that he knew who she was.

'She is probably very lonely and bitter,' he said,
'and needs more attention than most. From now on
I will go out of my way to be nice to her.'

Joe has gone to England with a pal for the duration
of the Summer holidays. It is hard to believe that he
will be a priest this time next year who was a small
boy only yesterday. Time passes quickly as we age.

An idea occurred to me a while ago. How about a
trip to Lourdes, just the two of us? Think on it and
let me know, but above all, for the love of God, take
things easy.

As ever,
Martin.

. . . .

The Dispensary,
Lochnanane.

Dear Father O'Mora,
I believe that we both have the interests of Mrs. Rosie
Monsey at heart. Since you exert a great influence on
her I would ask you to encourage her to use contraceptives, especially as her husband has become himself
once more. I will gladly supply these and all that
remains is for us to work out the form they should
take.

Sincerely,
Moffy, M.B.

. . . .

The Presbytery,
Lochnanane.

Dear Joe,

The missioners have come and gone but the number of
confessions shows a sharp drop. Neither were there the
usual throngs at the evening services. It could be television. Whatever it is the mission is losing its appeal.
I went to my first mission with my father at the age
of fourteen. We were there a half hour beforehand in
order to be sure of our seats. The church was mobbed
every night because there hadn't been a mission in the
parish for years and anyway it was a great diversion
in a country place. Our parish priest was a very out-
spoken sceptic who had no time for missions or missioners. He was Canon Mocky Leen. He would stand
at the back of the church taking in every word. The
missioner was a fat, red-faced man from Limerick.
His first two sentences terrified us. He gave a descrip-
tion of hell that had us shuddering with dread. His
voice was like thunder, almost deafening. Suddenly
Mocky interrupted him.

'You'll have to lower your voice my good man,' he
called, 'or you'll break the windows.' The missioner
was astonished but he lowered his voice.

On the third night of the mission which, incidentally,
is known as dirt-track night among missioners, the
sermon was about company keeping. Canon Mocky
as usual was at the back of the church holding a
watching brief.

The missioner warned couples who kept company
that it would have to stop, that he would not give
absolution to those who courted alone on dark nights.
Again Mocky interrupted.

'You'll never put a stop to it,' he called, 'better than
you tried it and failed. 'Twill always be going on. Sure
if it doesn't go on,' he proceeded, 'there will be no
missioners because there will be no one left to make
them.'

The missioner went on to deal with the dangers of

close dancing. 'Do not let your bellies touch when you dance,' he warned.

'He wants ye to dance back to back,' Mocky explained.

On the final night when the devil was denounced by a thousand throats the missioner announced that he was going to speak about vocations.

'Pray for a vocation,' he pleaded. 'Get your brothers and sisters and your fathers and mothers to pray for vocations for you. The church needs you.'

'Hold it . . . hold it right there,' called Mocky who was listening intently at the back of the church.

'What's this I hear?' he shouted. 'Listen to me,' he lowered his voice. 'If you want to be priests pray for your vocations yourselves and be sure 'tis a vocation you have and not a foolish notion put into your head by your mother.'

The missioner was about to continue but Mocky lifted his hand indicating that he had more to say.

'There are two kind of priests,' he declared. 'There are the priests who make themselves and the kind who are made by their mothers. The second crowd are no use to God or man. I've seen them myself meggegging like puck goats around Ballybunion and Bundoran.'

Mocky was great fun. Next week or so I'll finish the funeral rehearsal story.

Look after yourself.

Your affectionate Uncle,
Martin O'Mora, P.P.

. . . .

Loafer's Lane,
Lochnanane.

Dear Father O'Mora,

The Monster arter striken agen. I lucky not my time. I die for sure if I carry anuther baby. The doctor tell me he has pils and other thins make it safe. I sed I ask you first. You the best friend I ever had. The Monster afraid of you but wont go next or ner the presbry for a millen.

Your fateful servant,
Rosie Monsey.

• • • • • • • • • • •

The Presbytery,
Lochnanane.

Dear Doctor Moffy,

What madness have you been putting into the head of Rosie Monsey. She is in her forty-fourth year with fourteen children hale and hearty and yet you want to come along and destroy the morals of a good Catholic mother after this length of time. Have you no sense of righteousness that you should want to make this good woman no better than a streetwalker?

It would be more in your line to fill her in thoroughly on the tried and proven rhythm method without resorting to unGodly and non-Catholic devices. She will never use your murderous concoctions.

Sincerely,
Martin O'Mora, P.P.

• • • • • • • • • •

The Dispensary,
Lochnanane.

Dear Father O'Mora,

I am gravely concerned about Rosie Monsey. You forget that her husband is an ignorant lout who does not know the meaning of rhythm methods. He couldn't even spell rhythm. His is a classic case of 'penis erectus non conscientiam habet.' Total sexual abstinence is also out of the question for I happen to know that he threatens her with violence. Please see your way to using common sense.

Sincerely,
Moffy, M.B.

. . . .

The Presbytery,
Lochnanane.

Dear Joe,

Glad to hear you are getting along so well over there. There is little from here except that Father Ray has had another series of attacks. Anyhow he has recovered and is resting at present. The new curate is an excellent fellow. He remembers you from Saint Unshin's. He is a great help to me and loves hard work. We get along marvellously.

Let us now return to Bosco McNelly's funeral rehearsal or, as others call it, the German invasion of Tooreenturk. All was carefully rehearsed for weeks under various committees but a sizeable firing squad could not be found. When all fruit failed Bosco went to the nearest army garrison and was received by a young lieutenant who told him that such a thing was out of the question. The young officer who is today one of the country's leading industrialists was intrigued and when he finished duty that evening drove straight to Tooreenturk. He promised Bosco that he would have a firing squad of four army men under his command ready on the day but that if word got out about it he would probably be courtmartialled. He insisted in paying the men out of his own pocket. He would arrange to be hidden with his contingent in a clump of laurel near the grave and would emerge with the order to fire at an agreed signal.

Eventually all was ready. It turned out to be a day that would never be forgotten in Tooreenturk. First came a riderless horse in the shape of a jackass. Bosco was riding the real horse to ensure that the rehearsal went off smoothly. The jackass, representing Bosco's riderless horse, was led by the parish clerk who wore surplice and soutane and carried a large brass crucifix. Next came two altar boys carrying incense thuribles. These wore mauve soutanes and yellow surplices. They were followed by the local football and hurling teams in togs, boots and vermilion jerseys. Then came the Children of Mary dressed in blue. They were followed by the Legion of Mary. Thereafter came several nuns and hot upon these the village sergeant and his force of two Civic Guards.

Next came the bands. The first was the local fife and drum and the second an imported brass and reed from the city of Cork. The fife and drum wore tartan kilts. The brass and reed wore peaked caps and uniforms which were sky blue in colour.

After the bands came the people of the parish of Tooreenturk and there were also large numbers from adjoining parishes who, having nothing better to do, came along in case they might miss something.

Here, there and everywhere was Bosco on his horse. At one moment he would be at the end of the parade. The next he would be at the front. The bands were silent since they had only one function which was to play the Dead March as soon as the main body of the huge procession was in the graveyard.

All moved smoothly and according to plan. The riderless horse, i.e. the jackass was very well behaved considering that his nether quarters often came in for a belt from the swinging thuribles of the altar boys. As the gates of the churchyard hove into view one could feel a sense of mounting excitement.

First in was the jackass led by the parish clerk. Unit by unit the others followed until both bands were inside the gates. Father Bosco McNelly spurred his mount to the head of the column and with uplifted hand brought it to a halt. There followed two minutes of absolute silence when suddenly Bosco lowered his hand and pointed imperiously to the leader of the brass and reed band. The drums of both bands rent the silence asunder. The jackass at the head of the column became uneasy and proved difficult to control. At the first sound of the brass he reared and brayed knocking the parish clerk to one side. The clerk rose bravely and endeavoured to contain him. He was knocked aside once more. Bosco caught hold of the bridle but the creature was too strong. He broke from Bosco's grip and galloped madly across the graveyard.

'Hi . . . Hi,' Bosco shouted after the crazy animal. Mistaking this for the signal the young lieutenant and his party of four uniformed soldiers leaped forth from their hiding-place in the laurels. Sharply the officer's commands rang out. The long procession was paralysed. The guns of the firing party were pointed in the direction of the leaders.

The members of the Children of Mary screamed. Fear and alarm showed on every face. Vainly Bosco tried to convey to the soldiers that the time had not yet come. It was all to no avail.

In the background a man's voice shouted hysterically 'it's the Germans.' Word spread like wildfire that there was a German invasion.

'Fire,' shouted the lieutenant. There was a thunderous and ragged volley of rifle fire. People fled in all directions. Confusion reigned. The horse bolted with Bosco in the saddle. Shrieking and screaming the great mass of people erupted from the churchyard on to the roadway where hundreds of others joined the retreat. In a matter of minutes the churchyard was deserted save for four bewildered soldiers, a puzzled lieutenant and a jackass, who was now grazing serenely near the Celtic Cross erected to the memory of Father Bosco McNelly. So ended his famous funeral rehearsal, or as many country folk still prefer to call it, the German invasion of Tooreenturk. When Bosco died a few years later he had a very modest funeral indeed but please God we shall look for him and find him In The Nurseries Of Heaven.

There are a thousand great stories if only I could remember them. I will try to recall a worthwhile one

from time to time. For the present God bless and keep
you. Want for nothing.

Your affectionate Uncle,
Martin O'Mora, P.P.

. . . .

The Presbytery,
Lockeen.

Dear Martin,

I am now wherever God saw fit to place me. I left
instructions with my solicitor that you were not to be
given this letter till death visited me. In life you were
my closest friend and this, in a sense, is my farewell
to you. My worldly possessions consist of four hundred
pounds and my small library which is worth consider-
ably more. You will pay for my funeral out of the cash.
Give what is left to the girl Bridget Day who once
confided to me that I wasn't cross at all. The library is
yours. I would want nobody else to have it. My car
goes to my curate. He deserves it. I have no living
relatives therefore no dependants.

I can think of nothing else to say. Goodbye old friend.

Yours in J.C.
Ray.

. . . .

The Dispensary,
Lochnanane.

Dear Father O'Mora,

Rosie Monsey died a few moments ago. I realise you
could not be here. Your curate rendered every assis-
tance. I want you to know that she would be alive today
to care for her children if she had been allowed the use
of contraceptives.

Hers is not an uncommon story but it is a tragic one and a heartbreaking one for her children. She found herself pregnant again and was terrified. Poor ignorant creature, she visited her vagina with slippery elm bark in an effort to arrest the development of the child. After some time there was a slight haemorrhage. Next day she complained that she wasn't well, that she thought she had a temperature but which of her family could she tell what she had done. If she had only sent for me.

During the night she raved with fever but still no attempt to call me. The following evening she went into a coma. It was then they decided to send for me. Her eldest daughter came and I guessed instinctively that Rosie Monsey was lost.

The minute I put my hand on her distended stomach I knew that there was no hope. Her death certificate will say that she died from widespread peritonitis but that is not altogether true because the Catholic church had a hand in it too as indeed it had a hand in the passing of many a fine, decent girl over the years. I am too sick at the thought of Rosie's death to say more.

Sincerely,
M. Moffy, M.B.

•   •   •   •   •   •   •   •   •   •   •

The Presbytery,
Lochnanane.

Dear Joe,
What a terrible week it has been. First Ray and then Rosie Monsey. I hardly know where I am. There was a letter from Moffy reproaching me for my attitude towards contraception. Even the curate looks at me askance. Maybe it's my imagination but I feel he would have no hesitation in permitting Rosie the use of contraceptives. I could never do this. It would be opposed to all I ever believed. There is a natural law and to flout

it is to flout God. Most of Rosie's children must go to an orphanage. I will do what I can but all the clergy and all the institutions in the world will not replace one mother. This fact will always haunt me. It is a terrible cross to carry but then I did not become a priest just to make decisions that might be transiently popular. God will judge me and I will fully accept that judgment.

I could go on about Ray and about Rosie but it would be pointless.

What I would like to say to you Joe is that it is never easy to be a good priest but it is doubly difficult at the present time with true values diminishing day by day, non-stop assaults on celibacy and every corner boy in the country criticising the Church's attitude on one thing or another. Time was when the corner boys would run from us at sight. They are but a few of the village curs that snap at the great caravan of Catholicism.

Over the past few years our authority has faded till it has almost disappeared. No one knows for sure when the rot began. I believe it all started with Pope John XXIII although it was not started by him. I think old John knew what he was doing when he adopted a liberal attitude. He knew that many would see this attitude as an opportunity to press claims for a softening of the Church's attitude on many controversial matters. John knew that his liberality and candour would blow through the corridors of the true faith like a fresh wind, driving before it in the fullness of time the weaklings and the wasters who do not belong so that while there may be smaller numbers only the strong and the resolute remain. Remember that if the position of the Church seems weak at present it is merely purging itself of malcontents and biding its time, as it were, for the re-assertion of its authority. That authority was never weaker than it is presently. That is why old, frosty fellows like myself have to stand firm in the face of what must often seem to be reasonable demands. That is why we dare not yield to catchcries.

We are the hard core Joe, brought up on the Code.

93

Our mission is to stand fast and to hold on no matter what. We may seem out of step right now and there are many who would say that the world shall not look upon our likes again. They are wrong for believe me Joe the world will whimper for the likes of us in the fullness of God's time.

THE END

LETTERS OF A SUCCESSFUL T.D.
John B. Keane

This bestseller takes a humourous peep at the correspondence of an Irish parliamentary deputy. Keane's eyes have fastened on the human weakness of a man who secured power through the ballot box, and uses it to ensure the comfort of his family and friends.

LETTERS OF AN IRISH PUBLICAN
John B. Keane

In this book we get a complete picture of life in Knockanee as seen through the eyes of a publican, Martin MacMeer. He relates his story to his friend Dan Stack who is a journalist. He records in a frank and factual way events like the cattle fair where the people 'came in from the hinterland with caps and ash-plants and long coats', and the cattle stood 'outside the doors of the houses in the public streets.'

Through his remarkable perception we 'get a tooth' for all the different characters whom he portrays with sympathy, understanding and wit. We are overwhelmed by the charms of the place where at times 'trivial incidents assume new proportions.' These incidents are exciting, gripping, hilarious, touching and uncomfortable.

LETTERS OF A LOVE-HUNGRY FARMER
John B. Keane

John B. Keane has introduced a new word into the English language — 'chastitute'. This is the story of a chastitute, i.e. a man who has never lain down with a woman for reasons which are fully disclosed within this book. It is the tale of a lonely man who will not humble himself to achieve his heart's desire, whose need for female companionship whines and whimpers throughout. Here are the hilarious sex escapades of John Bosco McLane culminating finally in one dreadful deed.

LETTERS OF A MATCHMAKER
John B. Keane

These are the letters of a country matchmaker faithfully recorded by John B. Keane, whose knowledge of matchmaking is second to none.

In these letters is revealed the unquenchable, insatiable longing that smoulders unseen under the mute, impassive faces of our batchelor brethren.

Comparisons may be odious but readers will find it fascinating to contrast the Irish matchmaking system with that of the 'Cumangettum Love Parlour' in Philadelphia. They will meet many unique characters from the Judas Jennies of New York to Finnuala Crust of Coomasahara who buried two giant-sized, sexless husbands but eventually found happiness with a pint-sized jockey from North Cork.

Send us your name and address if you would like to receive our complete catalogue of books of Irish Interest.

THE MERCIER PRESS
4 Bridge Street, Cork, Ireland